LOVE WITHOUT

## ALSO BY JERRY STAHL

*Permanent Midnight*
*Perv—A Love Story*
*Plainclothes Naked*
*I, Fatty*

# LOVE WITHOUT

## STORIES BY

# JERRY STAHL

 OPEN CITY BOOKS

New York

*Printed in the United States of America*

These stories were previously published as follows: "Cossack Justice," "The Somnambulist's Wife," and "Jigsaw Music" in *Quarry West* (1979–80); "I'm Dick Felder!" and "Finnegan's Waikiki" in *Playboy* (1985–86); "The Age of Love" in the anthology *Unnatural Disasters* (1996); "Twilight of the Stooges" in the anthology *The Cocaine Chronicles* (2005); "Gordito" in *Open City* (2006); "L'il Dickens" in *LA Weekly* (2007).

Design by Nick Stone
Cover photograph by Carlo Mollino, untitled Polaroid, late-1960s. Collection of Rob Beyer. Courtesy Museo Casa Mollino-Torino. Author photograph by Frank Delia.

Library of Congress Control Number: 2007927001
ISBN-10: 1-890447-45-5
ISBN-13: 978-1-890447-45-8

OPEN CITY BOOKS
270 Lafayette Street
New York, NY 10012
www.opencity.org

Paperback Original
07 08 09 10 11   10 9 8 7 6 5 4 3 2 1

Open City Books are published by Open City, Inc., a nonprofit corporation.

*For M. S.*

# TABLE OF CONTENTS

# THE AGE OF LOVE

Her husband invented panty shields.

"They're going to be very big," she told me. "Bob used to say, 'Create a need, then push the solution.'"

This was 1969. I was fourteen years old. We were sitting next to each other on a plane from Pittsburgh to San Francisco. I had no idea what she was talking about.

Doris later told me she was forty. But I couldn't tell. When I first saw her, in the airport lounge, it was from the back. She was bent over a lady in a wheelchair, giving her a goodbye kiss. By chance I gazed over at this tableau. I was instantly entranced by the view under her rising hem. My eyes followed hungrily up over the backs of her thighs, under her girdle to a thrilling darkness the mere thought of which had me craning my head right and left to see if any other passengers saw me peeking.

At fourteen, a virgin and chronic masturbator, I knew I could file away this glimpse and call up the memory of those mysterious creamy thighs for unlimited sessions of self-abuse in the months and years to come. At that age, I don't know that I expected to ever even have sex. It was enough, really, just to have actually, almost, gotten a peek of the exalted area. Which may explain my alarm when the woman stood up, looked my way, and turned out to be my mother's age.

I wasn't sure whether I should still be excited. Or if the lines in her face should somehow cancel out the thrill I felt at nearly seeing between her legs. She wore butterfly glasses, another Mom-like detail, and a neck-scarf printed over with little penguins. It was all very confusing. I felt my face flush into hot red blotches. For the first time in my life I wondered if I might be perverted. Though I wasn't entirely sure what a pervert was.

To disguise my discomfort, I pretended to read my hardback copy of *The Call of the Wild*. It was a Bar Mitzvah gift from my grandmother. By now I was convinced the entire waiting room was staring at me, that everyone in the immediate vicinity was whispering about the young boy who got a boner looking up a skirt that might have been his mom's.

It would not have surprised me, at that moment, if some kind of Erection Police swooped into gate number four, guns drawn, led by some burly old veteran with a bullhorn who broadcast the situation to the folks on hand. "It's all right, ladies and gentlemen. It's all right. . . . We've got a lad here who seems to be aroused by the sight of a heinie that could belong to his mother. . . . We'll take care of it, folks. We've seen a thousand punks like him."

When I ventured to glance up again, I noticed that she'd been joined by a couple her age. I knew at once that the woman was her sister, and the man probably her brother-in-law. Both ladies wore their reddish hair brushed up in the back and down in the front, like Lucille Ball. The husband, who seemed to be a real joker, sported a short-sleeve Steelers shirt and arms so dense with hair I could see it from my seat. I wondered, for the millionth time, when *my* arms would start sprouting such a crop. Until recently, I hadn't been hairy anywhere, and it tormented me.

The husband leaned down to the old lady and made a face—bug-eyed, tongue-wagging—and both his wife and the lady I'd peeked at broke into gales of helpless, showy laughter. Except that my lady, as I'd already begun to call her, did not really seem to be enjoying herself. She chain-smoked, she kept looking all over the place, and her two hands never stopped touching, as if the one had to constantly remind the other that it was not alone.

When our glances met, for the briefest second, there was a nervous, almost hysterical quality to her grin. Her lips made a show of mirth, but her eyes glimmered with a desperation I could recognize. It was all so clear.

*She's not married. They're sorry for her. She's joking around to hide how bad she feels.*

Of course, I knew that feeling. That's how I felt all the time. As I sat there, pretending to read Jack London, spying on Mr. and Mrs. Hairy Arms, on old Moms in the wheelchair, and on my secret soul mate, the Unhappy Girdle Woman, this sense of knowing exactly how she felt—how different, how ashamed, how uncomfortable—was absolutely overwhelming.

I didn't even realize I was staring until *The Call of the Wild* clattered to the floor.

There were a few reasons my parents wanted to send me to California. But only one that the three of us could actually speak about. My sister Trudy had moved to Berkeley the previous year with her husband, Vance, and everybody thought it would be nice if I went for a couple weeks to visit.

The truth behind this sentiment was not so nice. My parents hated their son-in-law. "Vance!" my mother had spit right up to the minute of their wedding. "What kind of name is Vance?"

It was her habit, when she loathed someone—which she did with alarming frequency—to find some innocuous detail and rant about it as the source of her boundless repulsion. "Forget that the boy looks like a sneak-thief with those little eyes of his," she'd holler from the bedroom. "Forget that he said *from day one* that he had no intention of getting a job. Forget that it broke your father's heart the day *that thing* married your sister. . . . *What kind of a name is Vance?*"

My sister had upped and married him, at twenty, after a two-year engagement to Larry, a brilliant, suit-wearing pre-law student from Syracuse my parents both adored. Larry was perfect son-in-law material.

In my twelve-year-old naïveté, even I did not understand what Trudy was thinking. Until one day, during one of our long-distance chats, she told me she broke it off when she realized Larry's hair was thinning. "I just didn't want to wake up beside a bald man in a suit," she said. "Would you?" I said that I wouldn't. Vance wore a Che Guevara T-shirt and holey bell-bottoms every day. He also supported an enormous ball of frizzy hair he called his "Jew-fro," and refused to cut it off for their wedding until my father gave him five hundred dollars. Over the years, the "haircut deal" proved another perennial in my mother's boudoir-shouting repertoire.

The truth is, my mother's bedroom habits were another reason for this trip. Along with the reconnaissance aspect—my parents' refusal to visit my sister now that she'd married Vance, and wanted to send me out to check up on them—was the fact that my mother had started "staying in" again.

"Staying in" was family code for not getting out of bed. For not washing up or getting dressed or doing much of anything but staying horizontal and shouting out peculiar comments or requests for food. My mother would lay in the dark for days at a time. After a while the room grew thick with her scent, a close, private muskiness that drove my father, if he was in town, to sleep downstairs on the couch. When he was on the road—he sold novelty items, supplying "Joke & Gag" stores as far away as Duluth or Buffalo—it was just me and Mom.

No matter what, during daylight hours, it fell to me to do bedroom duty. "Bring me a peach!" she'd croak from the pungent dark. If I had a friend over after school, I'd smart from embarrassment at having to stop playing and hop to for this creepy, disembodied voice. Upstairs, with the drapes shut against the afternoon sun, she would throw back the blankets, instantly filling the air with great gusts of Momness. "Wanna cuddle? Wanna play Mommy's little boy like we used to?"

"I didn't know anybody else was home," the friend would say when I came back down. Then he'd look at me in that way people look at you when something's off, when something's wrong in a way that you don't want to talk about. "Is that your mother? Is she sick, is that why it smells?" And whatever I'd say, whatever I'd come up with as a cover, they'd always treat me a little differently the next day in school. I didn't have a lot of friends.

Sometimes a whole year went by without my mother "staying in." But now she was doing it again.

And it was worse than ever. My father told me she'd be going "on vacation" soon. Which meant another visit to Western Psychiatric.

This seemed like a good time to get on a plane and visit Trudy in California.

When we finally boarded, it didn't even surprise me that she was 21-F and I was 21-E. She had the window and I had the aisle. Long before we took off, the heat from her leg was so intense that I leaned her way, feigning boyish fascination in the weedy runway, just to see if I was imagining the oven-like warmth or if she were really burning. What I felt, when I let my right thigh graze accidentally against her left, was an even higher centigrade than I imagined.

My seatmate pressed back at once. As possessed as I was by sudden interest in runway activities, she edged against me and craned her neck to take in the cart piled high with Samsonite. Still not speaking, we both pretended utter absorption in the sluggish hand-to-hand loading of each suitcase into the hold.

I could hardly believe what was happening. My whole body shook with excitement. I had to clamp my jaw shut to keep my teeth from chattering. Drawing on some heretofore undreamed of reservoir of nerve, a reserve of untested manliness, I risked still more pressure.

This time my maneuver was blatant. I not only jammed my limb lengthwise against hers, I let my hand dip casually off the armrest, until my little finger dangled against her thigh. To my astonishment, her response was just as bold. The flesh of her hip under her drip-dry dress seemed to stream right through my stiff white Levi's. But that was nothing. Still facing the porthole—baggage-handling was just so fascinating!— she settled her left hand atop my right, pushing downward, so that my initial, timid exploration was hurtled instantly into another dimension.

For a moment, I had to hold my breath to fight off the excited tremors that threatened to slide me out of my seat in a complete swoon. My neck was so stiff I thought it would snap. I had my hand up her wash 'n' wear dress. Clamped between her warm, thin thighs, my fingers jammed against what felt like a moist slice of toast. Toast wrapped in nylon.

To counter this dizzy arousal, I drew back from the window and studied the unlikely object of my desire. Up close, I noticed, her scalp was visible through her auburn hair. I didn't think that women could go bald, yet had to wonder if she might be even older than I suspected. Her hands, too, were less than pretty, the backs showing raised veins that looked puffy and a little blue. Yet even if there was something old ladyish about her, it didn't matter. I'd never been so close to touching a girl—let alone a grown woman—"down there" as I was now. A state of affairs made all the more tempestuous by the fact neither of us acknowledged what we were doing.

Our limbs now jammed together from flank to ankle, I took the liberty of canting my face still nearer, until I could breathe her heat, the way you would a humidifier placed in the room to fend off croup. She smelled vaguely of camphor, an odor I recognized from having to rub Bag Balm on my schnauzer's teats after she'd suckled puppies. Camphor was Bag Balm's main ingredient, and I found myself stirred anew at the prospect of rubbing the pungent emollient on my neighbor at first sign of a flare-up. If the truth be told, I'd even been a little aroused at rubbing the stuff on Queenie. But this was better. This was a thousand times better, and we hadn't even taken off yet.

By takeoff, I'd managed to hook a finger over the elastic lip of her girdle, somewhere in the waist area, engaging a patch of skin that felt taut and fiery.

It was then I noticed that I had an audience.

One row up, across the aisle, a heavyset old man in bifocals was twisted completely around in his seat. He stared back at us, horrified. Unable to peel his eyes from my seatmate's parted knees. You could tell he wanted to say something, but didn't know what. He kept opening his mouth, then closing it again, like a goldfish.

I decided to look nonchalant. As nonchalant as any fourteen-year-old with half his arm up the dress of a woman old enough to be his mother could. This just made the old guy more furious. He tore off his glasses and scowled. He began clearing his throat, very loudly, all the while keeping his irate gaze fixed on my offending paw, I began to fear someone else would notice. I imagined how they'd turn around, somebody would see them, then *they'd* start staring, and so on, until finally the whole plane was shouting and pointing. For all I knew, the stewardess could arrest me, the captain could drag me off to some secret airplane cell, maybe behind the toilet, where I'd stay locked up until we landed in San Francisco and the FBI scooped me up to ship me back to Pittsburgh. I could already hear my mother, barking down from the bedroom to my Dad when she saw me on the news. *"Herman, I always knew that boy was sick!"*

To my infinite relief, the gaping senior finally turned away. But no sooner did I relax than he spun back around, this time accompanied by the apple-cheeked crone to his right. Side by side, they looked like the Wilsons, the next-door neighbors on *Dennis the Menace.* If Mr. and Mrs. Wilson caught Dennis the Menace masturbating, I was sure, they'd have worn the same looks of shock and disappointment.

As I stared back, I felt like two different people— cracked by the opposing entities that had slugged it out inside me my whole life. The split was clearest in school. From first grade on, straight As were matched by straight Fs in discipline. Watching the shocked old man and his wife, the A-making half of me was mortified. But the F-half would have liked nothing better than to cause a couple of heart attacks.

"Bob never cared," she said.

"What?"

I was so stunned to hear her speak that my hand popped free. For a second I just sat there, staring at the thin red band where the elastic had bit into my wrist. Then I eased under her dress again, like a small animal heading for its burrow.

She turned from the window with a little smile. Her tone had been matter of fact. But when she looked at me she seemed to get nervous again. Her face broke into the expression she wore with the people at the air-port, like she was just about to laugh or scream and had no idea which it would be.

"Oh sorry," she said. "Bob was the husband. I'm Doris."

"Doris," I repeated, like a man mouthing an unfa-miliar language. Up close her eyes were a startling blue. "I'm, uh, Larry," I lied, and for some reason her face relaxed.

I glanced back at the fuming seniors, but, to my relief, they'd turned toward the front again.

Doris checked, too, then aimed those strange eyes back at me.

"What I'm saying, Bob never cared," she began again. "About people, whatever, what they thought. Like when he went to see his project supervisor at

Johnson & Johnson to pitch them on shields. Bob invented them, you know. Panty shields were his baby all the way."

She stopped, awaiting my reaction, though I was still fuzzy on the particulars. I pictured something like gladiators used to fend off spears, only smaller, and lodged somewhere south of the border. Then my fingers made their way back to the toast-barrier, and Doris smiled.

"That's right. That's one of the originals. I still have all the prototypes. It's my way of keeping him here, with me. I think he would have wanted it that way."

Again she awaited my reaction, again I was afraid I came up short. "That's . . . that's beautiful," I said. It seemed like the right time to quote Rod McKuen or something. My sister'd given me one of his books for my last birthday, but all I could remember was the title. "*Listen to the Warm*," I said.

It was the most grown-up thing I'd ever uttered. Doris shook her head and smiled gratefully. She was old, maybe older than my mother, but at the same time there was something young about her. I noticed for the first time the way her lipstick formed a kind of ready-made kiss on her mouth.

Doris pressed her legs together, and once again I was shocked by the heat against my flattened palm, and that faint whiff of camphor. I got an erection again, but there was something different about it. I felt all kinds of things at once. For all I knew I was falling in love.

My face blotched up red again, but she didn't say anything.

"The J&J guys looked at him like he was nuts." Her voice had gone a little husky. "Some of them were actually mad. *Off-ended.*"

She paused, resting her head of Lucille Ball hair against the airplane window, and I ventured an exploratory probe in an untried direction, toward her thigh, away from Bob's prototype. I soon found myself yanking back a rugged strand of elastic and feeling something I'd never felt before. Something I'd only dreamed about feeling. Feeling *hair.*

"Mmmph," sighed Doris, shifting slightly, guiding my arm with her thighs. "Ten little men in pinstripe suits at a teak table the size of Guam. And you know what he said? 'If you boys don't know why this product is gonna make you a million dollars, I feel sorry for you. You've obviously got some very unhappy gals back at the ranch.' Do you believe it?"

I said I did, though this wasn't exactly true. I'd missed something, even though I'd heard everything she said. I felt fourteen again. On top of which I was getting really turned on from where she'd steered my hand—and the fact that she was the one who steered it there. Try as I might, I could only picture the shield as a kind of sewer lid, and I knew that wasn't right either. I wondered if they were hand painted, maybe even tie-dyed. As I was thinking, I felt my way along the side of the shield, past that tingly patch of fur, to what felt like a ridge of warm meringue.

I'd never done this before. I didn't know what happened to women when they got aroused. I'd never aroused one. I didn't know they got wet. Or if that was some kind of a problem. My fourteen-year-old mind was trying to wrap itself around things it pretended to comprehend and didn't.

As I listened for clues, I kept my fingers moving. I felt like a man doing an appendectomy out of a textbook.

Doris got a dreamy look as she talked. The plane had hit some kind of turbulence but I barely noticed. "It was important to Bob, see, that this was a positive product. Not, you know, something girls are going to buy because they've got some discharge. That's what the Board didn't get. They thought it was just for girls to handle their flow. Girls who didn't want the bulk of a heavy napkin. Girls with some condition that requires insulation!"

"Insulation," I repeated, when I realized she was waiting for a reply. My father, the novelty marketeer, had been passing along tips on What Makes a Top Salesman since I was three. One of his favorites was, "If you don't know what to say next, repeat what the other fellow just said." Until this, I'd never had occasion to use any of his advice. We weren't very close. But now that I'd taken a tip, and it worked, I wished I could call him up and

thank him. "Insulation," I marched out again, adding
"*huh!*" this time. Doris ate it up.

"Exactly!" she cried, absolutely beaming. When she
beamed she didn't look old at all. It was confusing.
"Exactly," she yelped again, pronouncing it "egg-
ZACK-ly" this time. Her voice was getting louder,
and I had to fight the urge to shush her. I had a thing
about public scenes, since my mother was always making them. The first emotion I remember having is
embarrassment—if that's an emotion. But Doris
preached on, oblivious. "Arousal is not some kind of
condition a girl has to treat—it's a treat a girl has to
condition! That's what Bob said. That's what panty
shields are all about!"

In the middle of this, I caught the head of the man
in front of us tilt to the side. As I hitched my seat belt,
*The Call of the Wild* slipped off my lap and landed up
the aisle, beside his brogans. This was before Doris had
plunked down. He made a show of reading the title,
then smacked a thick red hand off the cover. "Good
book, son. Good clean book." That's when I saw the
priest collar.

The priest's face, I noticed, was almost as red as his
hand. Especially the nose, which close-up was pocked
and dotted with tiny hairs, like a large strawberry. I said
I like the book, too, though in fact I hadn't got past
page one. *That* I read about forty times, unable to concentrate after my secret undie peek.

"More young people your age should read good books like this."

"Yes, Father," I said. I'd never called anybody "Father" in my life, including my own father, who was always "Dad." But I wanted the priest to think I was Catholic. I wanted him to like me, though I wasn't sure why.

"And you," he announced, as if he'd given the matter serious thought and come to this lofty conclusion, "are a fine young boy. A fine young boy." He gave my hand a little squeeze and handed over the book. "Aren't you?"

"Well, yeah. I mean SURE!" I blurted, half-shouting though he was only inches away. I did not feel like a fine boy. I felt like some kind of sex criminal. But I didn't tell that to the priest.

He nodded, despite my sputtering response, and tapped me on the head, gently mussing my Brylcreemed-but-still-frizzy hair. Now here I was, a mere hour or so later, shattering my good-boy image, chatting about panty apparatus with a strange female.

I watched the priest's skull rotate slowly to the right, like some hairy radar device, until his ear was aimed at us.

I don't know how I fell asleep. I had a dream that Queenie gave birth to pups on my lap. Except that the puppies kept sneaking back in. I had to search around inside her to try and find them. My hand was soaking.

I was scared. But whenever I looked down, there was
Queenie, gazing up at me with her grateful Schnauzer
eyes, her little pink tongue hanging out, panting away.
Instead of a collar, she had a penguin scarf around her
neck. I remember thinking, in the dream, *I really love
this dog. I love her more than my parents.* But then something happened. I couldn't get in. There was a shield,
but it was invisible, like in the Johnson's Wax commer-
cials. "Bullets bounce off!" said the announcer. And
suddenly my arms were empty.

I woke up hugging Doris. More than hugging,
holding onto her. Squeezing, the way my mother used
to when she wanted me to play "cuddle boy." When she
was staying in, and it was afternoon forever, and I had
to lay in her seething bed, my face in the hollow of her
throat, cheek mashed to her bosom, gulping hot,
under-the-blanket fumes until my eyes watered and I
pretended I had to go to the bathroom and ran away.

"I'm going to call you 'Dreamy,'" Doris laughed
when I blinked up at her. Something was different. I
tried to disengage myself but she said she wouldn't let
me. She wrapped her arms around mine, so that I
looked up at her at an angle, from under her chin.

Finally I realized. "You did something. Your hair . . .
it's—"

"Step aside Judy Collins!"

"Judy Collins," I repeated dumbly, eyeing the glossy
tresses that now fell over her shoulders. When you
don't know what to say, say the last thing they said.

"Like it?" she asked.

"Well . . . yeah! I really do!" Of course, I would have lied to make her feel good. But I didn't have to. Even though I remembered my mother once carping that women should not have long hair after forty unless they were witches. Mom was full of these rules, just like Dad had a million tips. But Mom had never met Doris—the mere thought made me shrink. The Judy Collins look was perfect.

I had to lean back and rub my eyes. For a second or two I couldn't take her in. Along with the folksinger hairdo, she'd managed to slip on a flower-print peasant dress, granny glasses, and love beads. There was even a peace sign decal on her forearm. She looked like she could be her own freaky daughter.

"Wow!" was all I could say. Somewhere under there was the nervous, unhappy, chain-smoking woman I'd spotted bent over a wheelchair at the Greater Pittsburgh Airport. But she was buried pretty far down.

"Are you, like, from San Francisco?" I asked.

"I am now," she said, a little loopily. This was when I noticed the trio of mini–Southern Comfort bottles peeking out of the magazine slot in front of her. "Bob would have wanted it that way." A chiffon hanky appeared in her hand, dabbing away tears. "I swear"— she pronounced it, lurching toward me for emphasis, "shwear"—"that man died of a broken spirit."

****

Doris, it turned out, had just come from her husband's funeral. The woman with the matching Lucille Ball hair was indeed her sister. But more than that, the jokey guy was Bob's baby brother, Bo. Bob and Bo had married Doris and Dot in a ceremony that got them national attention. Allen Funt, of *Candid Camera*, actually filmed the ceremony for an episode of his own short-lived *Candid* spin-off, *You Won't Believe This!* But the show, she said, was canceled before their double wedding made it on the air.

"Story of our life," she sighed, reaching for the third of her Southern Comforts to pour into her glass of Coke. "I used to tease Bob that we should change our last name to Almost, 'cause of all the stuff that almost happened. And all the stuff that did happen that almost didn't."

She stopped talking then and looked at me a little tearily. Everybody else on the plane seemed to be asleep or numb. The only overhead lights left on were hers and mine. Even the priest appeared to have given up his eavesdropping, having nodded off with his head still askew, his hairy ear positioned for maximum intake.

There was no sound but the hum of the engines that carried us through the night. The plastic glass was in her hand but she wasn't drinking any.

"Could I have some of that?" I asked, before I knew I was going to.

Doris gave a chuckle. Even her laugh seemed different in her hippie get-up. "Are you a juvenile delinquent? How old are you?"

"Almost old enough."

"Well, why not?" she said, offering the drink with two hands, to keep it steady. "What I've just been through, I should get everybody on this tin trap drunk. Including the pilot!"

With this she grabbed the glass back and took a swig.

"First the bastards didn't want the thing, then they stole the patent. They made him jump through hoops, then they shot him in midair. Murder in the boardroom, baby. If old Bob had a shield over his heart, he might still be alive."

Doris let out a long sigh and handed me the drink again. There was almost enough left for a whole gulp.

"I thought it was 'The Summer of Love,'" I said. "That's what they called it in *Newsweek*."

"Don't think small," said Doris. "It's the whole damn age. Howzabout I teach you how to love right now so you'll be ready for it? So you won't have to do any catching up later?"

"That sounds all right."

"Well, don't fall off your seat or anything."

"It sounds great, really. I think everybody else is asleep."

"Pretending," she mumbled, and slowly raised her arms for me to come closer. "Everybody's probably watching right now and wishing they were you."

"Well, jeez . . ."

I felt my throat go dry and couldn't think of anything else to say. I hoped it was too dark for her to see my face flush up. I was already beginning to shake a little. I wondered if my whole life I'd start to twitch whenever things got exciting with a woman. But then, I figured, they'd probably never get this exciting again.

# COSSACK JUSTICE

When Raymond was eight, his mother cured him of stealing by hiding a mannequin's hand in her purse. It was a Tuesday, after four. Raymond's after-school ritual had just begun. First a loud *"Mom!"* at the front door— to make sure she wasn't home—then a dash up the stairs, five double steps, three at once at the very top, down the hall with his large eyes on his own skinny image approaching in the dresser mirror, straight for the top drawer where his mother's change purse lay tucked in the cup of a black brassiere.

Raymond dipped his arm into the ocean of cool silk. He touched the soft suede like a treasure on the bottom, unsnapped it, slipped two fingers inside and felt for the familiar wad. He inhaled her perfume and held his breath. But instead of a dollar bill, he pulled out a hand.

A tiny hand. His throat made a little-bird noise and his knees turned to vapor. Aunt Helen found him curled up on the carpet, his fingers white-knuckled around the wooden palm. She scooped him up in her heavy arms, said, "He's here! He's up here hiding!" and Raymond woke to find himself aloft for the first time in years. Half asleep, he felt for an instant what he felt as a baby.

Aunt Helen let him down. "What happens now?" she shouted. Her husband Jack ran into the room behind her. "Does he know or doesn't he?" he asked quietly. "When do we tell him?"

Raymond sensed with great relief that they were not talking about stealing. But he knew he would not do it any more. "Your mother's left us," said Aunt Helen. She looked past him, staring in an abstract way at the pink hand in the tangle of her sister's lingerie. "Left us what?" asked the boy, trying to piece things together. "What did she leave us?"

At the school where Aunt Helen and Uncle Jack sent him, the counselor kept tropical fish. Raymond saw the counselor twice a day. Each morning, when he entered the mahogany-walled office, Dr. Boerner stood hunched over one of his tanks. His short gray hair ceased in a sharp line over his collar. Half-moons of skin showed over his ears, what the boys called "whitewalls."

"Come look at this one, Raymond."

He did not turn around when he spoke. He seemed to talk backwards. (*The hand . . . I believe . . . in dreams it bothers you?*) His words sounded in a slow, choppy way, and Raymond sensed they were full of hidden tricks. The counselor did not look at him.

"The blue one, with the white speckles . . . gorgeous, isn't she? Gorgeous . . . Her babies, those little dots you can hardly see, she eats them. Do we like her or don't we?"

"She's still pretty, even though," Raymond said.

He did not care for the fish. While Dr. Boerner went on and on, Raymond stared at his own reflection in the glass. The same thought passed through him, day after day, as he stood side-by-side with the doctor. The same feeling. He remembered his face, exactly how it looked on the day he found the hand. He always remembered rushing down the hall, his eyes on the mirror in the bedroom. A red blotch flushed his chest when he recalled it. Since then everything had changed. He'd lived with Aunt Helen and Uncle Jack for a summer, then they brought him to this school and left him there.

Nothing changed. When he thought about his eyes and how he used to feel before sinking his arm in the drawer—it was still the same. He was in her bedroom, his hand in the silken deep. That was how things were supposed to be: at home, after school, with a dollar for comic books and supper at seven when his mother came home from work. All the rest was just what had happened, the different things that were not part of this real thing underneath.

He listened to Dr. Boerner tell a story about barnacles. He watched his face in the dark glass without moving.

Raymond's roommate, Gavin Soussloff, was the son of a Russian prince. His ears were tiny and white as scallops; his wrists so slender, his small chest so delicate he did not have to attend many classes. At night, Gavin and Raymond roamed the empty classrooms together. They crossed the wide lawn of the quad in total blackness, their arms slung loosely around each other's shoulders.

Gavin knew the school's bowels. He had been there for two years before Raymond, since the age of seven. He knew all the passageways. He knew which doors were left unlocked by the old night watchman, Mr. Smythe. Sometimes they followed the old man, along catwalks, down marble stairs, into the vaulted chapel made huge by night.

Smythe's rounds took them in and out of a thousand darkened niches, like a treasure hunt. The two boys crouched in corners, waiting for the old man to pass. When they heard him muttering, the click of his key in the time clock he carried on his hip, they both held their breath. The old watchman was crazy, Gavin said. He had read every book in the library. Raymond said no, he couldn't believe that, but Gavin insisted. To prove it, one night Gavin whistled from a landing in Weschler Hall, and Smythe stopped on the steps.

"That you?"

"It's me," said Gavin, running up to the watchman. Raymond trailed cautiously behind. He discovered the two were some sort of friends.

"Who's your buddy, then?" Smythe's voice was scratchy and high-pitched, an old man's croak.

"Just Raymond, a new boy this year."

"That so?"

Smythe touched Raymond under the chin, his fingers dry and thick as rope. He let his hand graze roughly over the boy's cheek. The light was gray, and Raymond could barely see his face. Smythe's glasses reflected the vague light in the stairwell. As Raymond squirmed, the watchman's eyes grew huge and then disappeared. He grunted. Raymond tried to break away, but the old man's hands were in his shoulders like claws.

"Be still," he growled.

The air around him smelled like asphalt, hot tar, impossible to breathe. He brought his large face closer. His lips were moist, white flecked. His breath whistled through his nose, wind in a storm. The sound grew louder and Raymond twisted in his grasp. He cried out, "Gavin!" But the other boy only giggled and said, "Smythie, how many books did you read in the library?"

"Them all. I read them all." The old man's voice cracked and trembled.

"Gavin?" Raymond shouted. *"Gavin!"*

His friend's laughter echoed down the stairwell.

****

Raymond spoke politely, as he'd been taught.

"Dr. Boerner, Uncle Jack. Uncle Jack, this is Dr. Boerner."

Aunt Helen beamed. "He does do his introductions like a little man."

Raymond stepped back while the adults shook hands. Uncle Jack combed his fingers through his hair when he let go. Dr. Boerner said, "Sit down, sit down," and his aunt and uncle said, "Thank you," at the same time. The counselor strode back behind his polished desk and cleared his throat.

"Raymond, would you like to remain in the office?" he asked gravely. "The boys," he explained to his guests, "we treat them . . . let them make their own decisions."

Raymond didn't answer. His eyes stared through themselves in the aquarium. He had a special thought, a private phrase he repeated in his mind like a prayer: *Pretty soon it will all be over.* . . . A blue fish fluttered through his vision to the light.

"He can stay," said his uncle. He looked from Raymond to his wife, and then at the counselor. "What that boy hasn't been through."

Dr. Boerner touched his tie and folded his hands in front of him. "Of course, the child has had a time. . . . We know. . . . The reason I asked you folks to come. . . ."

"Oh, he's coming along," Aunt Helen blurted. "He's a perfect little man."

Talky-cocky. If he slipped into the right pants pocket of his suit, Raymond could feel his testicles. Gavin had shown him this trick. One night they stayed up to slit secret holes inside their trousers. Gavin said that in Russia soldiers wore fur drawers. On guard duty, they warmed their fingers, holding their little marble men.

The counselor's drone stopped and started. "I asked you folks to come . . . the reason . . ."

Gavin also had a string of worry beads from Turkey, which he showed Raymond how to use. "Turks need the beads," he explained, "because they don't have testicles. A Russian puts his hand in his pocket to think."

Raymond loved this story. He stood off by the softly gurgling tank, feigning interest in the fish, thinking about Gavin. The adults' words floated back and forth behind him: ". . . *traumatic . . . watchman . . . withdrawal.*" He waited. Aunt Helen moaned, "Oh God."

Eyes on his own eyes, a smile hidden in his lips, Raymond busied his fingers with his marble men. He was a Russian soldier. His uncle's hand settled on his shoulder like a dove.

Gavin was all packed. His father, the prince, had hanged himself. Raymond heard about it in chapel, and skipped out during the hymn. He returned to find his frail roommate sitting on his trunk, leafing through a book on backgammon. Soussloff Senior had brought the game to America. Raymond wondered if Gavin knew his father had killed himself, or if he thought the playboy had simply died. He climbed up on the bed and sat beside him on the trunk.

"Coming back?" he asked.

"The year's almost over."

Raymond nodded. He took a cigarette from the silver case he'd boosted from the headmaster, offered one to his friend. Everyone else would still be in chapel; they were safe.

Gavin's side of the room was already bare. Where his sable pelt had been mounted on the wall, the yellow shone a shade paler. Raymond already felt deserted. The empty walls and shelves seemed to amplify the silence.

"Well, now we're both orphies," he said finally. "You've made the grade."

"Free, white, and ten," Gavin added without a smile.

Raymond slid closer, until his hand just touched the fringe of Gavin's pocket. The flannel—regulation little-boy gray—scratched lightly on his knuckles. He wormed in a finger.

"Do you want me to do it?"

Gavin leaned back his head, blowing smoke rings at the swirls on the ceiling. "A normal function of the prepubescent phase," he recited, "mutual genital manipulation need not be cause for alarm."

"I know," said Raymond.

He reached through the slit in his friend's right pocket and palmed what there was to palm. He squeezed the marble men.

"Did I ever tell you about Cossack Justice?" asked Gavin. "How the Cossacks used to test young boys they captured in battle? If they couldn't piss over a horse's back, they threw them off a cliff."

"And if they could?"

Gavin leaped down from the trunk. "They threw them off a cliff."

# GORDITO

All Puray ever talked about was Zelda Fitzgerald. It was kind of creepy, but I've listened to sadder insanity.

"Zelda used to do this thing with carrots, I swear. She'd braise them, get them just a little hot and tender, then slide them in."

I didn't have to ask where. But I did anyway.

"Do you have olive oil?" she asked. "I can show you. Sometimes I sprinkle cayenne."

I suppose I should tell you now, Puray was a little person. Pre-PC, a midget. A stacked half-pint. Knee-high. But where do you put *that* in the story? March it out in the first sentence, then that's what it's about. It's one of those hot sexy midget stories. Then you make the associations. Stereotypes. Male midgets are massively hung. They all look like thumbs. Ignorance. Or not.

But march the news out in the middle—*"And, by the way, the love of my life was genetically predisposed to never make forty inches"*—and what is that—O. Henry?

The least important detail was her stature. It was her Zelda thing. How much she wanted alcohol, more or less constantly. I once asked her why she drank. She said, "My father was in the circus."

"And—?"

"There is no *and!* Slide the carrot in real slow. Put the right music on. *Like there is any right music.*"

When she was being dramatic, her eyes would bug out. Frida Kahlo–adjacent. The unibrow made her more beautiful. She was half Guatemalan, half Armenian.

"A sultry mix, Daddy used to say, but unduly hirsute."

After the circus, her father wrestled. She showed me a poster that first day, while she braised.

*"GORDITO!"* The name in flaming letters across the bottom.

His expression was weirdly subdued. He had a professorial look, despite the leopard-skin toga, and a creased forehead like his daughter.

"He could have been a doctor of literature in Guatemala City. But, of course, his size. No one wanted to hear about Henry James from a tiny hombre who looked like Mickey Rooney, but smaller, darker. Mickey Rooney with machismo. Do you know why I was his favorite?"

There were probably a dozen answers to that I didn't want to hear.

"Because I was dangerous," she said, letting that hang in the air for a while. "To myself."

This was the kind of thing she said. The kind of thing that stirred feelings inside me I'd never had before. Like I wanted to kill her and take care of her at the same time. Like love was something foul you had to wipe off or extract with tweezers. Sometimes I saw the space over her head as tainted. What she gave off was so powerful it stained the air. But it wasn't a smell, exactly. It was absence. All the space she didn't take up: the grease-stained wall behind her, where a normal woman's breasts would be. How can I explain this? When her friends came over, I felt hulking. I didn't see them as small. I saw myself as an embarrassment of size.

"Some men think Puray is a little doll," she whispers, her voice raspy as an old black man's. "They want to play with Puray and dress her up. Bounce Puray on their knees."

"That's because they've never *had* you on their knee."

Our little joke. Puray's flesh had some density that makes her heavy as a standard human. I don't know the physiological explanation, but despite her stunted height, I could barely lift her. It's as if she was condensed. Hypersolid. After sex she liked to slap her ass and holler, "pig iron." Or when she'd been fucked *and* fucked up, "pig irony." For her the joke was fresh every time. She'd giggle her throaty giggle and hop in my lap, her leaden shanks nearly driving me through the floor.

Once, at a bus stop on Figueroa, she finished off a short dog of schnapps some rummy had left in a paper bag, then leaped up, balanced herself on the back of the bench, lifted her pink skirt high enough to show baby-blue thong, and stage dived into my lap. The impact was like a sandbag, dropped from a great height onto my femurs. But the pain was made small by the image preceding it: the robin's-egg ribbon buried in her black thatch, pubic hair thick as Castro's beard. Only slightly matted. She had good hygiene, she just sometimes forgot to finish what she started. I've seen nastier things. I just can't remember because of the hole this one burned through my medulla longata.

In the grips of some passion spaz, I grabbed her by the hair and yanked her face up to mine. I just wanted to stare at her, then kiss her. Mistaking my advance for attack, Puray slid a blade out of her bra and slashed. She missed my face but caught the hand I'd swung in front, what we know is called a defensive wound from TV cop shows. I saw my fingertip fly somewhere under the bus bench and, without thinking, I smacked her. Or tried to. She'd done some novelty boxing, and ducked me easily, so my fist crashed into Plexiglas. Apparently, my scream softened her up. She slipped the blade back in her bra and just slapped me.

I still wanted to punch her, but saw the eyes of the taquería patrons across the street. It was lunch hour.

You don't know shame until you've fought with a female little person in public. Punch a pretty midget in the face, see the stares you get. When she kissed me, shame coursed through my system like bad speed, making me excited and nauseous all at once.

"Do you love me?"

Her eyes glazed when she got this hot. Violence got her like that. But it had to be accidental. She could tell the difference. If she ever thought I was faking—playing mad 'cause mad got her hot—she came right at me.

"You only like me because I make you feel big."

She knew just where to slide the knife.

On an old-fashioned mercury thermometer, Puray Magic Marked a slash at her normal temperature: 99.9. Half conscious on booze and party pills, she'd tell me stories about being a child in freak shows. Her skull, more or less normal size now, had reached adult diameter by her fifth birthday. Which made her resemble, in her own words, a hydrocephalic toddler with a swagger. Gordito dressed her in a matching leopard-skin mini-toga, safety pinned, like his, at the left shoulder. When she was nine a lady from the Department of Health offered her mother twenty-five dollars not to breed any more. That was the going rate for handicap tube-tying.

"My mother was nearly six feet, and stacked. Daddy called her Mt. Olympus. He'd climb her with a knife in his teeth." (The same one, it turned out, that she'd tried to filet my face with at the bus stop. It was a family heirloom, originally stolen from the Times Square Howard Johnson's.)

"Daddy overheard the D.O.H. lady talking to my mother and went into Gordito mode. He told her I wasn't handicapped. Even at nine, I felt redeemed. I thought he was sticking up for us. For the family. And then I heard him say, *I know the rules. Non-handicap gets fifty.*' Hah! I learned everything I needed to learn about life, right there."

I loved the brazenness of her nightmare history. There was no gray area. My mother made me cuddle naked till I was eleven. But she didn't put me in a sideshow with Lobster Boy. I had certain advantages. Puray believed, more than anything, that her past connected her to Zelda's. When the future Mrs. Fitzgerald was ten, she telephoned the Montgomery police department to tell them a child was in danger of falling from the roof of a building. Then she climbed out her third-story window and onto the roof, waiting naked for their arrival. Her father was on the Alabama Supreme Court, so the house was big.

"Even then, Zel understood," Puray muttered, in her fetching slur.

"Understood what?"

"What do you think? You don't need to get drunk to indulge in irrational behavior. You need to get drunk so you can explain it."

Puray braised her carrots every morning. It was what she did, instead of vitamins. We lived in a studio apartment near the corner of Normandie and Sunset. Little Armenia. The tiny kitchen area was full of potted plants. None of the plants seemed to die, but none of them looked healthy. Unless they were supposed to be yellow. The first time we met, she told me she had hepatitis, on and off. *"Liver stuff, so we should be careful—if you want to be careful."* It occurred to me that she might have given the houseplants hepatitis, if such a thing were botanically possible. I didn't want to find out. I'd seen what she could do with a root vegetable.

Our days passed simply. "I'm sleepy because of the hep," Puray would yawn, no more than two or three hours after rising. Up at ten, back in bed by noon. The good hours she spent in a high chair at the three-legged kitchen table, writing in legal pads. When she wrote she made sucking noises with her lips and ate compulsively. Her prose resembled Zelda's only at a distance. Mostly it involved drinking and losing control, in no particular order. Our first month together, she showed me her memoir, *What Are You Looking At?* It had an arresting beginning. *"Sometimes little Cinderella dropped a load in a blackout. . . ."*

Puray could not decide whether to refer to herself as Little Cinderella or Teeny Zelda. But names weren't the issue. I thought "load" was little crude, but it wasn't just that.

"Blackout loads?" I said with as much tact as I could muster. "I think that's something I'd have noticed."

Puray didn't see anything strange. "When a girl's survived as long as I have, she learns a few tricks."

But I wasn't buying it. "Some things even a trained professional can't hide."

"Wanna bet?" She barely bothered to sneer. "Ever wonder why I menstruate five times a month? Why I sleep with a pad in my panties? Maybe it's not a pad!"

Since she didn't like to be touched while sleeping, she might not have been lying. We never had sex in bed. Besides which, I wasn't sure I wanted to know.

We shared a Murphy bed, which unfolded to the lip of the bathtub separating the tiny living area from the kitchen proper. Puray day-napped in the tub. Around 10 A.M. her lids would start closing. She'd climb the stepladder to the raised tub, equipped with a dog bed. It was a perfect fit.

"Brain fog," she'd sigh when I tucked her in. "This Mami needs sleepy-sleepy." We kept the shades down, so it was only daytime in a technical sense.

If what Puray said is true, Zelda undid her husband with her carrot routine. In front of the maid. In front of the mailman. In front of Hemingway, who called her Flapper Sadista.

"The miracle was that it never appeared in a story. Though of course it does, in subtext. . . . Zelda liked it, right up in *here*. Mmmmff . . . and sometimes *here* . . .

You want to hold this? *Mmmm.* Easy, like you're cleaning a pencil sharpener. Daddy liked vegetables, too."

When it got good she kind of sang, in a whisper. *Gordito!*

I know about mutants. The women they end up with. Women you want in private.

When what you get is a Puray.

You get a mutant, beautiful or not. And you love them. Because they're just like you.

"The secret," she said, "is you never peel them. You leave them dirty."

# THE SOMNAMBULIST'S WIFE

Last night at three George made love to me like a human cannonball. His hands were hot and his eyes were open. He said, "Sadie, baby doll, I love you," even though my name's not Sadie and I am not sure how he really feels.

I never knew what to do when the strangeness hit. It started three years ago, at Daddy's house, one night when we went to bed early after a long dinner and a big fight.

Daddy had called George a lout. He told him what he thought of white guys in the ring, especially white guys blind in one eye. Like always, George couldn't do a thing but take it. We both knew he'd break Daddy in little pieces if he ever touched him. All tucked in there in his wheelchair, Daddy looked like the Wizard of Oz. The blanket came right up to his chin. You could see his arms, but there was something about the way the blanket just lay there across his chest, the way it sort of folded down under and dropped to nothing, that let you know what kind of shape he was in. "Even my stumps got stumps," he'd say, almost like he was proud of his condition. Daddy used to wear a flag from right under his armpits to the floor, but the man from the VA said it was probably against the law. "What if it rains," he said, "and you get caught outside wrapped up in the stars and stripes? Right there, you're breaking the law."

Whenever you mentioned the man from the VA, Daddy'd spit on the carpet, like an outlaw. But he took off the flag and started wearing the blanket me and George got him at the plaid stamp redemption center. One-and-a-half-books.

I wondered who the hell this Sadie was, but I knew better than to ask. I got my first hint of strangeness that time at Daddy's, when George got up at dawn and relieved himself downstairs on the good sofa. I followed him. At first light George sat right up beside me, putting on his little slippers. For so large a man it was wondrous how tiny his feet were. George said it was a blessing in the ring but I didn't see why. The sofa was special in our family. It belonged to a great aunt, who got it from her husband's hotel. I wanted to stop him but I couldn't. I had to watch. Without so much as a sigh, George reached down and lifted up a cushion, then he took out his organ and made water like it was natural. When he finished, he shook himself good and put the cushion back down.

By this time I couldn't keep quiet, but I spoke real gently so as not to startle him or wake Daddy. "George, honey, are you feeling kind of funny?"

"No," he said, "it's just that goddamn Rolling Rock of your father's. All that fresh goddamn mountain water."

He came back up and dozed in my arms, a contented, childlike smile on his face. I couldn't even clean up until noon, but lucky for us Daddy only used the sitting room for company.

George has had three fights in two months and lost two from falling down in the fourth round. I could tell he wasn't hit; he just dropped. The second time it happened I asked if someone was paying him to go down. "I wish," he said. His last fight was last night at the Elk's. He clobbered a fellow called the Black Pope so badly they had to put five stitches in the Pope's nose. There was a lot of blood, but it wasn't terrible. And it was good to see George winning.

Mr. Mackey, George's trainer, presented him with forty dollars plus ten bonus. I wanted to celebrate, but when we got home George fell asleep in a chair with his clothes on. Around three I dragged him to bed, where he woke up howling mad. "You little termite," he sputtered, "you didn't even wake me! I missed the fight!"

He shot downstairs to the phone and tried to dial Mackey. It wasn't until I brought out the fifty, still wrapped up, that he calmed down. "Well, I'll be switched," he said. "Never mind," he said, putting down the phone. He smiled so I could see his two gold molars.

"I have a crick," he said. "Rub me down."

That's what he always said when he wanted affection. We went back upstairs and I doused him with gin and smacked his neck and shoulders.

"Are you thinking what I'm thinking?" he asked.

"What's that?"

"I'd like to go a few rounds right now."

Sometimes it got him going to talk kind of sporty.

"I want to go to the ropes with you-know-who. I want to clinch."

By now I knew all the signs. "Call off your dogs," I said, and went for the helmet. I felt silly, but when he'd get like this I had to put on the helmet. If he felt too good he'd get carried away and start to cocoa-butt. He'd hold me around the neck and pop his forehead right into my own. I liked the rough stuff, in a way, but not the cocoa-butts. My helmet said Steelers, George's favorite, and he'd twist right up and romance through the chin guard. I loved him, in a way, but it was all so cruel and different from what I imagined when I was a girl, lying in bed and watching Clark Gable blow smoke rings on the moon. It's not that it was so bad, it just wasn't what I expected.

****

Elmira was the only person in the world I could tell about George. Her Hal had a cancer on his backside the size of a baked potato, and he said he wouldn't do a thing about it until the fall. In the fall, he said he'd be damned if he wouldn't wait until winter, and meanwhile the spud kept getting bigger. I figured George's problem would even out the stories about Hal's potato, even though Elmira exaggerated. Lots of times Hal came over for a snort with George and I couldn't see any lump on his backside. But Elmira said he knew how to hide it.

For the longest time, I thought about getting George to see the Reverend Vic Delaney. I thought maybe it could help his sleep and personality problem. I told Elmira: "I've seen him cure old biddies who could hardly shuffle up to the pulpit. Some of it has to be real or they'd shut him down."

Elmira, who was more religious than me, who'd load the Dodge on Sunday and go off to church with her boys, said she thought it might be a real aid. "He's the man with God in his handshake," she said, just like the announcer on *Reverend Vic's Crusade*.

To make it pleasant, I suggested Elmira take her Hal. I said it would be easier to hook George if all four of us went together, and it couldn't hurt. "It would be fun," I said, "like doubling up at the drive-in, like the time we all saw *Shane* at the U-Do-It."

"It's a thought," she said, fussing with the hanky at her wrist. Elmira always kept a hanky, either stuffed up her sleeve or down her bosom. "The thing is," she said, "I'd have to make a promise. That's the way our marriage works. If Hal promises to paint the den, I have to promise to visit his mother in the home and say he has the flu. It's an arrangement. When I got myself a permanent, he got me three nights in a row with the lights on and my skirt over my head on the kitchen table."

"Is that bad?" I asked.

"It gets worse," said Elmira, "just touching that big old cancer is worse."

After our candid chat all I saw of Elmira was her head at the kitchen window at dusk when she did the dishes. For a few days I watched her kitchen until the lights went off, but nothing ever happened. Meanwhile, George was stirring himself up for another fight, a bout with Prince Dixon, who had already tagged him twice. In bed, George's body hummed like a big heater. I warmed my toes against his thighs. All night he stared at the ceiling, and sometimes I looked right in his eye and made crazy faces, but he didn't flinch.

The night before the fight, I wanted badly to have relations. George said his gut muscles hurt from sit-ups. I said I would sit on him, and George said his groin ached from jumping rope. After that, he rolled onto his stomach, then over on his back. He stared straight up like *Gone with the Wind* was playing on the ceiling, and he hadn't already seen it five times.

When it got so my skin was hot all over my body, I leaned close and whispered: "George, it's Sadie. It's your Sadie, George." At first nothing happened, then George's tongue peeped out between his lips. It sort of slithered out while I repeated that awful name. "It's Sadie, George. . . ." Once I even called him "Georgey," which I know he hates, but he just smiled in his child-like way.

It was a pleasure just to touch George when he was so easy about it, when he was asleep. I stroked his head and brushed my fingers along the back of his neck, a spot we called *puppybrush* on Doreen's baby brother when we were little. After he got a fresh crew cut, all the girls wanted to touch that special spot, to rub his puppybrush. George didn't mind. After I had my fill, I let my lips drift to his forehead. I had never done him like this. I just touched my lips to George's face while he stayed all quiet. Right then, it was perfect: every-thing we had. I felt myself so relaxed in love I passed from hot right over into cool. We had all the time in the world. When George mumbled "Sadie," I said *"Yes, yes!"* and pressed my lips down all over him.

In the morning I asked George if he remembered any-thing about the night before. "I think I dreamed about a fish," he said. I wondered if the dream was a good one, and he allowed that the fish was very happy. "The dream made me perspire," he said, "and I woke up wet and hungry."

"Me, too," I said. While he did his sit-ups, I fixed pancakes with bacon and eggs. Then George said he felt like a burger if we had any frozen. He had two. It seemed like we both felt pretty good. Usually, before a fight, George's appetite would shrivel up. Everything would shrivel up. By the day of the event he'd be so nervous that he couldn't put words together and whatever he'd eat would come back up. Within eight hours, George was going up against Prince Dixon, who had pounded his ribs and defeated him before, but he was still eating. When he finished, he wiped his mouth and kissed me on the lips. It felt so natural, my own luck scared me. He might not have known it was me.

I was still tingling when Elmira popped in and told me they'd found another lump on Hal. This one was on his side. Now that he was convinced he was a sick person, Hal agreed to go see a doctor before Easter.

Elmira promised to pack him picnic lunches for a week if he went sooner. Hal said *two* weeks. "I would have said forget it," said Elmira, "but I remembered us talking about Reverend Vic. We agreed he could skip the doctor and I'd put rice pudding in his lunch for ten days."

I didn't get it.

"He'll get healed at the Crusade," she said. "No picnics."

In the second round George smashed Prince Dixon's jaw so badly his left ear dropped an inch lower than his right. The Prince kept swinging and caught George with a wild left to the temple. It was almost an accident. The temple was George's soft spot.

"The Prince gave him a kiss with that one," said Mackey. The trainer stood right beside me, chewing on his panatela. He always stopped by for a minute or two during the bout. "The sound of that smack gave me a headache," he said. George's eyes rolled back in his skull, and when they came down his face flushed the color of wet newsprint and he walked in tiny circles. "Go get him!" Mackey shouted. "Go get him!" When George didn't respond, Mackey gave up and spoke in a normal tone. "Confidentially, he's gone water rat," he said. "I hate to watch."

Right then the oddest thing happened. Daddy came rolling down the aisle with L'il Bit, his nurse, and stopped beside me. "Shit," he said, by way of greeting. "How are you?" I replied. I'd never known Daddy to attend one of George's fights, though he always called when he lost. For the occasion he was back to wearing his flag. L'il Bit rolled him right over my feet, crushing my white pumps. "Mackey," he said, "what's wrong with that boy?" "He's a rodent," Mackey replied. I could tell by the way George stood there blinking that he was gone. For all he knew, he was sitting on the edge of our comfy bed, deciding whether to stretch out or snuggle back in. I knew his mind: the crowd did not exist, there were no lights; he floated in foam rubber in his own warm mind. We all watched while George held out his arms and looked down at his trunks like he was surprised at what he was wearing. He hugged himself and Daddy spit on the floor. "I don't even like the boy," he said, "but this is disgusting."

While the ref counted off, Prince Dixon hopped from foot to foot and popped his gloves together. The bell rang and George just stood there. Prince Dixon grinned through his shattered jaw. Daddy cracked L'il Bit with his quirt and lashed out at the crowd, trying to make it to ringside so he could spit at George. Some days that was his passion. When Daddy lived in the V. A. hospital, he and the other multiples got together in the afternoon around a spittoon. It was something they could all do. A fellow didn't need arms and legs to join in. Daddy and one man, a Major Biddle from Greensboro, South Carolina, got so good they held a special olympics, a spit-off, and raised three hundred dollars in assorted bets. The staff at the VA thought the activity helped morale, which tends to be pretty low among amps. Daddy considered himself an athlete, something he never was before he lost his limbs. In his declining years, this experience turned out to be one of the most rewarding of his entire life. "One thing I know," he liked to say, "is the thrill of competition. No guts, no glory."

Distance, not aim, was Daddy's forte. From a few feet below the ring he let fly at George and stained

Prince Dixon's royal blue trunks. The Prince's trainer had witnessed the old man's feat, and he said something to his boy. They both left in a hurry, with George stumbling behind before Daddy could work up another shot. The only targets left were strangers, people he had no reason to get, and Daddy never had much truck with random violence.

Not long after the Prince Dixon fiasco, George took me out to Howard Johnson's. I got the burger plate but George ordered trout because it was fish night. After a little cajoling, I got George to admit he had some kind of problem, though he wouldn't believe the things I said he'd done. The flooding of Daddy's sofa still shook him up. "I'll go see the Reverend," he said, forking out the bones, "but you've got to guarantee he won't make me sing in front of people."

"Guaranteed," I said. The burger was dry as hair. "I never saw Vic Delaney make a person sing, but I've heard he can make cripples dance."

"That's different," said George. He had no patience and put a huge piece of fish in his mouth with the bones still in it.

"Are you thinking what I'm thinking?" he asked.

"What's that?"

"Let's take your Daddy. I'd love to see that old fart strut."

"George," I said.

He tried to grin and show his molars but the trout needles scraped his throat and he started to make noises. The waitress, a straw-haired little girl with "Bernice" on her tag, came over and asked if we'd like more water. "How about rolls?" she asked. George was coughing and it made her nervous. He made hoarse, gasping noises trying to get his breath. "Who's Sadie?" I said.

George sounded like a bad clutch. I reached over the table and gave him one on the back and he came around. "How 'bout more butter?" said Bernice. This was her station and it didn't look right. "Go away," I said. This was it. "Sadie was my mother," said George. "You know I never lied to you."

"Let's have Bloody Marys," I said. I hardly drink at all, but when I do, Bloody Marys are all I drink. "There is no need to be ashamed," I said. George looked stricken.

"But I never met her," he said. "She's just a name stuck in my mind."

I felt myself getting clammy down under and knew that after one Bloody Mary I would want one more. It would soften up the burger. I told George that I understood, I always understood, and his furrowed brow shone smooth as a boy's once again. In his relief, George began to spin the tale of Sadie, whether as daytime or nighttime truth I couldn't say.

It started, he said, when Sadie left him with three aunts to run off with an exterminator. She had two other sons, also abandoned; one of George's stepbrothers was a Little Rock city councilman. But the worst was the latest development. A year and a half ago he spotted her picture among the post office WANTED flyers: "Sadie Kiner, alias Joanne Silk, alias Maura Wilmette." He thought she looked a little like him around the eyes, with a shrunken face.

"Mail fraud," he said. "I don't even know for sure what that is."

"It's not that bad," I said. "No one gets hurt."

George was fighting off tears and not paying any attention. "I still think about her," he said.

"She'll always be your mother."

I felt sad about the whole business and wanted to get something nice for dessert. George was sniffling. He ordered lemon pie and I chose the apple brown betty. George cut his pie in two and gave me half, and I spooned out some betty. "The cost of batteries today," said a man at the next table, "and it don't pay to send the boys down with flashlights." For some reason, this made my skin crawl. I wanted to gargle with something that would kill all the germs in my brain.

"Good pie," said George. "I feel like I could go the distance right now."

Vic Delaney sent us personalized greetings and six tickets for his Easter Crusade. Hal had already died, of a heart attack, but Elmira still wanted to come along. Lately she had taken to quoting her own home-baked scripture. She dabbed constantly at her eyes with her hankies. "We're all just lambs on the freeway," she said. I wanted to make sure Vic handled what George had, but there was no way of knowing. Elmira and I studied the evangelist's picture in the little circular that came with the tickets. He reminded me of John Garfield. There were also pictures of people from all over who had been healed. In the bottom right-hand corner was a pleasant-looking lady in a uniform holding a pair of crutches over her head. "No more crutches for El Paso Woman!" said the caption. "As Reverend Delaney ministered, something began to happen to PFC Helen Furth. God was touching her body and completely healing her arthritic knee. It was a very happy Helen Furth that hurried forward to give her testimony. SHE WAS NO LONGER LEANING ON HER CRUTCHES—SHE WAS SWINGING THEM. 'I can use these crutches for firewood,' she said."

"Smile upon us!" said Elmira when we finished reading. Everything she said sounded biblical. It had happened since the funeral. She now carried three handkerchiefs, one up each sleeve and one between her breasts. "I can talk to Hal through my mood ring," she said. "The Chinese call them 'blush stones,' from the cheek of Jesus."

I no longer enjoyed our morning talks. Elmira was too preachy and I had my own problems. It was me who sent off for tickets and made plans for the whole Crusade. I decided we could bake up a chicken and eat it cold on the way. We could pick up George at the plant and go directly. There was only one problem: Elmira wanted to take B. Q. and Wesley, her boys, and I wanted to take Daddy and his nurse. "We'll just show up and they'll let the extras in," I said. Elmira thought about that and decided it was all right. "They're good Christians that run the arena." On the big day, Elmira put on a new face. For the first time since Hal's burial, she wore a colored dress. George was wearing his sport coat, but he had to put it on top of his work smell, and it had been hanging all day in his musty locker at the plant.

"Nobody will notice," I told him, because he was so worried about it. B. Q., Elmira's twelve-year-old, said he wished he had a clothespin. "B. M. to you," said Wesley, the little one, which Elmira claimed is how he pronounced "me, too."

Almost as soon as George got in the car, he fell dead out of it. I wasn't sure what to do. If I woke him, he would blow up and howl; if I left him he could start making wild small talk to invisible souls. There'd be some embarrassment. If it happens, I thought to myself, be ready! If George began talking violent, I would say: "Listen, children, this man has a special problem and that's why I'm taking him to the Crusade." I hung on to that for a while, but as we were driving I felt bad about making any excuses at all. I wouldn't say that, I would say, "Get out of the car, all of you," and then we would have to drive to Mexico, or some place where no one would know. I'd work my fingers to the bone to keep George hidden.

We sat in traffic for fifteen minutes, and it took fifteen minutes to drive to the arena once cars started moving. B. Q. and Wesley said they had been there the month before, to see a hockey game, and I hoped they would keep talking about that, maybe fight about it, so they wouldn't notice any muttering from George. By now his eyes had popped open and I wished I'd remembered to bring his dark wraparounds. The back of his head rested against the seat and his mouth drooped open, sagging lower on the right. He looked like a reminder to give to the less fortunate, someone who stared at an eclipse or witnessed the means of his own demise.

The arena was just in sight when George started up.

"Hal," he said, soft at first, then a little louder, "hey, Hal, what's it like up in heaven . . . up there where the trees don't have no shadows?"

"Oh, God," I said. "Please stop that!" George said his piece and cackled in a low way I never heard before. The kids in the back seat giggled and stopped. I could not bear to look at Elmira, though she knew George was given to these things when he slept. I snuck a glance at George and he looked peaceful again, not all twisted up and sorry. It was like the time he fell asleep in my arms at Daddy's house, after puddling the sofa, and smiled like a boy. For a second he reminded me of young Monty Clift, whom I loved as a girl. He didn't say any more. At a red light I watched him hard, and the sweet smile wore off. The car in front of us was full of blond boys in white shirts, and it made me wonder. If there were five of them, how many had what George had? Which ones lived with that time bomb that exploded with words and strangeness when they became men? One out of how many? All the boys looked normal from behind.

"George had himself a dream," I said, just to break up the silence and my own thoughts.

"Did I?" he asked, now full awake. "I don't remember."

He chuckled and turned around to Elmira. "You look nice," he said. He joked with the boys, "Cat got your elbow or something?"

In the rearview, Elmira smiled in a funny way. "And kings shall be fools, and fools kings," she said. "This too shall pass."

She went on like that for the rest of the drive.

When I was a girl, I used to think the sky was painted with invisible paint. Something hovered behind it, something greater and still more invisible than the great blue secret. There were no edges. I wondered what happened if the magic spilled. If bits of sky landed on your head when you were walking home from school, they turned you the color of sidewalk, or you became a little cloud with eyes. I wondered, where was George when his mouth talked and his good eye drilled the air in front of him? His right pupil was milked over and I thought that, maybe, when he was going on in his state, he saw through that one. That milky spot was like a cloud floating on a broken-down horizon, blocking out a sun that gave no light and never moved. I thought: what he sees is invisible.

Maybe the only time he was really with me was when he slept.

We pulled up at an appliance store and George got out first to help Elmira. "You're a gentleman," she said, as if nothing had happened in the car. "So was my husband." George just smiled, showing his teeth. The two boys were quarreling. "Daddy's dead. That means he doesn't have to eat," said one. "You die if you don't eat," said the other. "You're stupid."

I was struck by how many folks were there to see Vic Delaney. Before this, of course, I had only seen the Crusade on TV, but when it's in your town and you actually attend, that's different. There were lots of families, mostly with a gawky daughter or two walking in back, and the brothers staying out ahead like they came on their own. At first, all the crippled unfortunates that we could see got off of the same bus. We saw it parked by a back entrance to the arena with the spastic and misshapen struggling down the two steps to concrete and then through the special gate. George said it was fine how they brought hospital folks up for the show.

My big worry was Daddy: people in wheelchairs made him nervous. He didn't think he was like them. It might have been all right if I'd brought a chicken leg for him to munch on but in the excitement I left the bird in the oven. Elmira was walking a ways ahead and I wanted to give her a laugh. "Absentminded is what I'm getting," I said, to cheer her up. "I'll probably burn the house down." She stopped dabbing her eyes for a second and dabbed mine, which I thought was sweet but gave me the heebie-jeebies when I thought about it later.

Crowds were extra hard for Daddy. He felt no shame about the chair, or that L'il Bit or someone else had to roll him around. What turned his blood were all the short fellows who now towered above him. "Look at that rummy," he would snort, pointing out some fat squirt in a red-and-white Corn Chex jacket. "If I'd have kept my frogs' legs, I would've made him sweat. Now the little turd thinks he's Edward G. Robinson."

On line outside our gate, George was all eyes. Something about the cripples hit him, like he had made it to the other side, and now he could turn around and savor all the ones who got cut up along the way. I began to notice what I didn't like. "You know," he said, "there is such a wide variety of personal tragedies to be had."

"I guess that's true," I said.

He nudged me, and I saw a young couple who shared a malady. Neither had much of a right arm. His stopped at the shoulder, like it had been torn off, and all she had was a small, spider-like hand peeping out of her blouse. The couple walked in step, with their heads held erect, as if marching. But as they rushed forward, it seemed like they were listing slightly to one side, as if being tugged or guided by the part of them that was not there. Or trying not to be.

"I wonder if they met at a club," said George, "you know?"

I was thinking: people wanted to be saved from different things. Most of the children showed up healthy, as did most everyone, except those whose fate it was to stand out in this lifetime. Most of all, you couldn't help but stare a little at the offspring of the lame and halt. There was the little girl who walked so slowly, stopping every few steps to wait while her stricken mama inches forward in her metal walker. The child's eyes stayed fixed on the ground ahead of her, gauging the inches still to be endured. I knew what they felt when Daddy plugged himself into the black machine, or breathed into the mask, or just lay there forever asking, "What did you learn in school today?" Tubes and blood were frightening, but not as bad as noises, which haunted the mind at night, and the low green smell of sickness in a house was the worst of all. This was what you took with you, in the skin. When I was very little, I used to brag to my girlfriends with their sturdy fathers, "Daddy knows how to dance with just his hands." And once, when I said it in front of him to show Doreen and Isabelle Reid, his face puffed up scarlet. Doreen started to cry and ran away, but Isabelle and I watched. Daddy made two fists and broke out in a wild, shaking cough that left him with a twitch. "That's not dancing," said Isabelle. And Daddy was so surprised he calmed down and said real soft that he had to think, and gave us both six cents for popsicles.

George said, "You know I never thought of it before, I can't figure out whether your amputees pray to God to make them whole, or just to make sure nothing else comes off."

We were supposed to meet Daddy in front of the hot dogs and pizza place, and before I saw him, George spotted his plaid blanket. "Would you look at that coot put it down," he said. Between the strolling families I saw Daddy chomping on a foot-long. L'il Bit had one, too, which meant he was in an expansive mood.

"Good evening," he said when we got to him. "How's the shell shock, or whatever it is?" he said to George. "Name one white man in the past ten years who had a chance in the ring."

"Don't start in," I said. "We've lost Elmira and the kids."

"They've gone on ahead," said Daddy. He gulped down the last of his dog and winked. "That ball park mustard goes right through me."

"Shall we go in?" I asked.

"Oh, well—*Jesus!*" Daddy's face went red, all of a sudden the sweat hit his lip. George gave a little hoot and I turned around. The door to the men's room was swung open and a huge limbless Negro, strapped onto sort of a sidewalk raft built over skatewheels, rolled toward us, smiling and excusing himself to the many people who had to step out of his way.

"Howdy," said the barrel-chested fellow when he came to Daddy. "I'd say you 'n' me in the same boat."

Daddy hardly looked at the man. Beneath the brim of his hat his face was paralyzed, but the raft man did not seem to mind. "You ought to get one of these," he continued, tapping his little platform, chuckling to himself like the whole thing was crazy but fun. "I can tell you where to get one and they got 'em in all sizes. Don't waste your time in medical supply joints 'cause they don't stock 'em. They'll just tell you to stick with the chair, that's that. That's *foolishness*," said the Negro, as if Daddy was trying to argue. "You go down to Kennedy's garage on the north side and you tell Red you a pal of Johnny's. They got a lot of these contraptions 'cause they use 'em to work under the trucks. You tell 'em Johnny sent you down."

The cripple filled his huge chest and nodded to all of us after his spiel. He said it was a fine night, especially fine to see the Reverend Delaney, and then he turned right and skated back into the crowd. Daddy's face shone white and damp below the boater.

"Did you see that?" said George. "Did you see that?" He was as happy as I'd ever seen him. "You should have thanked that fellow. Now you can get yourself one of those, play with the kids on their skateboards. I almost wish I could try one of those myself."

George gave another hoot and chuckle, and Daddy snapped his fingers for L'il Bit to take him. He spit hard on the ground and went off. "Rows E–10 and –11," I called after him.

By now the organ had started up and you could feel the bass notes out in the concession area. "That's the same one they use to play *Charge!* on hockey nights," said George. He was happier still, and I felt the glumness just swallow me up. It was like a trap door had opened under me and I hadn't stopped falling, had just discovered I even was falling. This was what I felt: my confusion. What George had was a revolving door. He walked in one person and walked out another, but he never dropped straight down, in his own soul, like I did. He was asleep.

Inside the arena things were starting up. Somehow, when I had thought about the Crusade, I had not thought about the sermons and the hymns and the responsive prayer. All I thought about was the part where Vic says, "Does anybody here want to be saved tonight?" And I had imagined that scene: George walking humbly to the pulpit, the multitudes watching this big man who stops before Reverend Vic and says, *"Sometimes I can't control it . . . make me one whole man."* That's what I imagined he would say.

"Come on," said George. "They got singers, too."

"I hear it," I said. "Onward Christian Soldiers."

If nothing works, I thought, I can always be like PFC Helen Furth, who threw away her ugly crutches and spun into Jesus' arms. It would be the last place they'd look, George or anybody. I had dropped down so far now that my head cleared. This was not that airy, crystal feeling. It was not like when I was a girl who watched the sky, and I could see the good in things so clear it was like there was nothing else. What I saw now was the dark.

George was standing at the open door to the arena, and all the people were singing and clapping with the choir. What they saw was the perfect truth. I had hauled George out to be cured, to be made himself, and here he was being himself, smiling at the music and the crowd and the many sights. The shadow of my doubt was so great that it swallowed the light, swallowed everything, so there was nothing else and the darkness seemed like truth. Are we ever anything but ourselves? When he hurt or ruined, when he collapsed or laughed or loved me in his odd way through some hollow dawn, I bent myself to the shape of his need. No matter who or what he was, I was transformed.

Just thinking so hard made my hands hard little fists. George was waiting, in silhouette, at the end of a short ramp on the topmost stair of the aisle. I stepped up close behind him and studied him, that tender skull. A high, amplified voice boomed throughout the arena: *Ladies and Gentlemen, welcome to this gathering of the blessed.* For a second, I looked at the temple, and then I flew toward it with the whole weight of my soul. *Sweet Jesus!* cried the voice, as George headed down the long, steep stairs that led to my salvation.

# JIGSAW MUSIC

Lorraine had lived in her new apartment for three months before meeting her neighbor, Mr. Carrigan. Often, at night, she had heard him doing things. From the high, whining sound she guessed that he was either drilling or using an electric mixer. But she never complained. Lorraine had been an only child in a quiet house. For her, a bit of racket in the dark hours was less of a disturbance than a balm, a sign of life.

When her job at the day-care center was over for the day, Lorraine liked to drive home with the tape deck in the Pinto playing loud. She went through phases: some weeks she cranked out the Stones and sang along with tunes she'd grown up with, others she blasted Mozart through the open windows. Lorraine liked it when the car beside her was playing music, too. She'd look at the driver, who would look at her, and then they'd both smile as they went their separate ways.

The day Mr. Carrigan met her in the apartment parking lot, her music was the first thing he mentioned. "I could hear you from half a block," he said. "Why so loud?"

Later, she would wonder what he was doing there in the first place. She would realize he was waiting. Lorraine had been playing Billie Holiday and was feeling mellow. She smiled and said the music helped her unwind.

"Everybody has to unwind," said Mr. Carrigan. "That's why I'm glad we're finally getting together."

Lorraine thought it was a funny way to describe meeting in the parking lot, *getting together*. But she liked the way the old man stood before her, his hands on the hips of his faded overalls, his face as hard and sullen as a Maine farmer's. The apartment complex was full of younger people, most of whom worked downtown but wanted to live a bit outside the city. It was odd to see Mr. Carrigan, a man of at least sixty, in the new development.

As if he thought she admired them, Mr. Carrigan said that he'd worn the same clothes for thirty years. "I never throw anything away," he said. "I wash them myself every Wednesday, and when something rips I sew it myself. I always have."

"That's nice," said Lorraine. "What do you do?"

The old man shook his head and a strand of thinning sandy hair flopped over one ear. "In my day, a person asked *How do you do?* Now they want to know how you pay for it."

"Just curious," said Lorraine. "I sometimes hear you working, through the walls. I just wondered what you were doing."

"Would you like to see?"

"Well, I don't know," said Lorraine. "I was going to go in and fix supper. Today I had to skip lunch at work."

"Just for a minute," said Mr. Carrigan.

Lorraine could think of no real reason to refuse. So she followed the old man up to the second tier of apartments. It felt a bit odd to walk past her own door to the one beside it, the source of all the sound that calmed her when her own thoughts kept her up at night.

"Here we are," said Mr. Carrigan. He pulled out a large key ring from a pocket on his chest. There were, Lorraine noticed, only two keys on the ring, and a chunk of cork dangling on a string. "Do you see this?" asked Mr. Carrigan, touching the cork. "This here's a fisherman's best friend. Drop your keys in the water and they float right to the top. Saves having to spend half your time bent over."

"Pretty clever," said Lorraine.

She wished she had at least stopped off at her own place, but now it was too late. Mr. Carrigan fussed with the bolt and then pushed in with his shoulder. "Here we are," he said again, sweeping into the living room. "Make yourself at home."

"My goodness," said Lorraine. She could not remember ever uttering the phrase before. While her host shuffled into the kitchen, she surveyed the small factory Mr. Carrigan had made of his apartment. It was shaped like hers: one large room with a hall branching off to a kitchen, bathroom, and small bedroom. But Mr. Carrigan had installed a large machine, what looked like a giant microscope with a blade jutting down where a lens would be. The thing sat in the center of the room, flanked by a pair of sawhorses and a stack of clean, white pine that gave the place a fresh smell.

"That's my best friend," said Mr. Carrigan, stepping back in the room with a tray and glasses. "That's my jigsaw. If they knew it was here I could get in hot water."

"Why?" asked Lorraine. "Is it illegal?"

"Light industry," said Mr. Carrigan. "It's a zoning thing."

"Oh," said Lorraine.

Now she would have a picture when she heard the sound. Now she'd know. She imagined him, at night, feeding the machine, hunched over the driving blade while the wood fell in simple designs to the plastic bucket propped up beside it. Dozens of wooden birds and Indian heads hung on Mr. Carrigan's walls. Some of the plaques he'd painted, and some were stained or shellacked.

"Do you sell them?" asked Lorraine.

"Once in a while," he said. "Would you like one?"

"Well," Lorraine said.

"Please," said Mr. Carrigan. "I have something here you'd like."

It seemed to Lorraine that he only pretended to look in the bucket near his workbench. In a second, he came up with a deep-stained, beveled heart the size of a pie.

"For you." He handed Lorraine the heart, and she saw her own name engraved along the bottom in swirling letters, like those on a greeting card. A pair of plump cherubs hovered above it.

Lorraine held the thing in her hands. "I don't know what to say."

Mr. Carrigan chuckled and touched his hair. "Let me get some wine," he said. "I have some my brother made five years ago. He liked music, too."

Lorraine tried to smile.

When he returned with the dark bottle, Mr. Carrigan set up two folding chairs. "Do you like the heart?" he asked.

"I do," said Lorraine. "I do. It's really something."

Mr. Carrigan, flushing slightly, poured two glasses of purplish wine. "I was saying," he said, "about my brother, he was one of the Pennsylvanians."

Lorraine still held the gift in her hands. When he handed her the glass of wine, she placed the heart gently on a sawhorse. "Who were the Pennsylvanians?" she asked.

"Fred Waring and the Pennsylvanians," said Mr. Carrigan, "they were Guy Lombardo's big rival for years, before Guy started playing the Waldorf things on New Year's."

"That's something," said Lorraine. The first taste of wine was like prune juice, but tainted. It was thick and bitter. "That's something," she said again, sliding forward on the metal seat.

"Of course," said Mr. Carrigan, "why should you care?"

"It's not that," said Lorraine, suddenly guilty. "I just have to go." Her own father was very old when she was young. When her father spoke to her, he always seemed embarrassed, as if he were not sure what a man his age was doing with such a young daughter. "I can stay another minute," Lorraine said, "but I have to go back and get ready. My boyfriend Roy is coming over later."

"The dark-haired boy?" asked Mr. Carrigan. "I've seen him."

"He's thirty," said Lorraine.

"Go if you want," said Mr. Carrigan, "but I'm having another glass in your honor."

"All right, one more," said Lorraine. "Just let me freshen up."

"Just down the hall," said her host.

Lorraine knew where everything was. The apartment was a mirror image of her own; their bathrooms shared the same pipes. When Mr. Carrigan showered, she could hear the water hitting the tub. She did not like to flush or run water when she thought of some-one so close, just on the other side of those thin walls.

When she sat down, Lorraine thought about Mr. Carrigan. He had a way of looking at her, squinting one eye, as if he forgot that she could see, too. She wondered if his wife had died, or if she had left him. If he had ever married at all. His bits of carpentry were all over the apartment. That was probably all he did with his life: pattern new little projects, then build them, one by one, and find somewhere in his little apartment to display them. Even the bathroom had a piece, a very small one, mounted high on the wall before her.

At first the little disk looked like a dab of paint. It might have been a charm, or a coin. It was stained mahogany brown and stood out sharply against the shiny white of the bathroom. As she washed her hands, Lorraine tried to get a closer look. The thing was less than a foot from the ceiling, no bigger than a quarter. Lorraine regarded it for a minute.

"Are you all right?" called Mr. Carrigan.

"Fine," said Lorraine. "I'll be out in a sec."

Lorraine wore tennis shoes to work. They were per-fect for standing on the edge of the tub, leaning over to look at the wooden curio. By keeping her left hand around the shower rod, she could reach it with her right.

She did not mean to remove the thing, but when she touched it the disk slipped off its tiny nook, into her hand. It felt like a wooden ginger snap. In the center of the piece Mr. Carrigan had etched a tiny heart, like the one he'd cut out for her. Lorraine held it for another second. It struck her that it might really have been an ancient coin, a talisman, when she happened to look up and see the hole.

A tiny hole. Just below the hook that fit into the wooden cookie, there was a hollow about the size of a dime. Lorraine leaned closer and slipped in her finger. It closed at the end, an inverted cone, coming to a point like a sharp pencil.

"Lorraine," cried Mr. Carrigan. "Lorraine!"

"Just a second."

She leaned a little farther, clutching the shower rod, and pressed her eye to the wall. The wall felt cool against her skin.

"Do you need anything?" Mr. Carrigan asked.

He seemed concerned that his guest had taken ill.

Lorraine answered that she was okay. But now she could see: a corner of her shower, part of her sink and the medicine cabinet mirror. She slipped the wooden disk back over the hole and stepped down to the floor. She ran the water for a second, automatically, then opened the door. Mr. Carrigan was waiting by the door.

"Do you want anything?" he asked. "Some Pepto Bismol?"

"I'll be okay," said Lorraine. "I think I'll be going."

Mr. Carrigan looked stricken. "*Now?*" he said, "why don't you want to sit down? Relax?"

"I should go," said Lorraine. She hurried through the living room. For the second time, she looked at the walls. They were cluttered with plaques and knick-knacks, the things Mr. Carrigan made with his machine.

"I'm still glad we met," said Mr. Carrigan. His hair, which had flipped back over his ear, now shone more gray than sandy. His face seemed paler. Lorraine mumbled something from the door. She wanted to be in her own apartment.

Mr. Carrigan stepped out with her and watched as she worked her keys in her own lock, unlocked the door. "Goodbye," he said.

Once alone, Lorraine did not look to either side of her. She walked straight through her living room and into her bedroom, the only room which did not share a wall with her neighbor. For a long time she sat on her bed, half-waiting for Roy to arrive before she came to any decision. She did not give any direct thought to what she had just discovered; she thought of her mother. Years ago, she had instructed Lorraine in what she called "lady things."

Her mother tried to educate her with tales of *what could happen.* She never spoke directly. She told Lorraine about a girl in her high school—she never had a name—who had been allowed to do bad things.

She had been *slovenly about herself*, said her mother. Because the girl was not *careful with her things*, the boys all knew her *secret thoughts*.

"*They can see you*," her mother said. "*They can see inside you*."

At the time, as a girl of nine or so, Lorraine did not know what her mother meant. But there was something, even then, very spooky about the thought, about having the boys see *inside* her. Lorraine grew up feeling that sometimes the men around her could see inside her, and that, when they did, it was her fault always, for being *slovenly about herself*.

Lorraine had just dozed off when the knocking woke her. For a fraction of a second she did not remember her neighbor, the pinprick in the bathroom wall. But, edging through the living room, she felt her neck flush and tingle. She had a sense of Mr. Carrigan, the old man squinting through the plaster. She had told him, she remembered, that her boyfriend would be coming over.

"Roy?" she said, opening the door.

"Hello," said Mr. Carrigan.

Lorraine jumped back. "What is it?"

"You forgot this," said the old man. He handed her the wooden heart.

"All right," said Lorraine. She took the gift and started to shut the door. But Mr. Carrigan took a step forward.

"One more thing," he said. Lorraine froze. Mr. Carrigan squinted and leaned toward her. She thought of the dark stain on his fingers. What had he seen? Mr. Carrigan smelled of shellac. "I was going to play my music," he said. "Would that be all right?"

"What?" said Lorraine.

"My music," he said, grinning his old man's grin. "I'm going to be working the jigsaw. When I want to relax, I like the noise."

"I don't care," said Lorraine.

"Just thought I'd ask," said Mr. Carrigan.

Lorraine started to close the door, when Roy stepped out of Mr. Carrigan's apartment. "Hi," he said, "I met your neighbor."

Both men laughed. Roy slapped the older fellow hard on the back. "I walked by and the door was open," he said. "He showed me his stuff."

"I fed him a ham sandwich," said Mr. Carrigan. "I hope you don't mind."

Lorraine stepped into the apartment. She heard Roy say so long to Mr. Carrigan. She was already in bed when he returned. She had undressed and slipped under the blankets.

"Honey," said Roy. He kneeled beside the bed and looked into her eyes. "Did you have a bad day with the kids? Mr. Carrigan said you had a chat."

"He makes those things," said Lorraine. She spoke into the pillow, so that her voice was muffled. "He uses them, on the walls."

"That's right," said Roy. "He's all right."

Roy took off his shirt. "I just want to hug you," he said. He wrapped his arms around her and lifted her up off the sheets.

"What are you doing?" asked Lorraine.

"I'm not ready for bed," said Roy. "Who's ready for bed?"

He carried her into the living room, onto the couch where they watched TV. "I want to play around in here."

"Please," said Lorraine.

"It's okay," said Roy, "sit on Daddy's lap."

While he hugged her she looked over Roy's shoulder at the wall.

"What did he show you?" Lorraine whispered. Her breasts swelled and tickled between his lips.

"Your little heart," he said.

The high, whining sound filled her apartment. Lorraine heard nothing at all until it stopped.

# I'M DICK FELDER!

For no apparent reason, Felder's son, on his tenth birthday, decided to change his name from Chuck to Shecky. The boy, whose main interest was plumbing equipment, gave no explanation. But he was so insistent that Felder went ahead and picked up the necessary forms at city hall one day after work, though he had no intention of actually mailing them off once the child had filled them out.

The Shecky-Chuck situation was just one new thing about his own life that Felder did not understand. Lately, there seemed to be more and more of them, such as why his wife, Gene—short for Eugenia—had suddenly become so feverish on their bed of matrimony. The pair had wed when Felder was fresh out of Colgate Dental and setting up his own practice. (Felder could never mention his alma mater without thinking of his father, a retired tool-and-die man. "How do you like that," Felder Sr. would joke each Thanksgiving when Felder came to visit. "The kid wants to be a dentist, so he picks a school they named after a toothpaste!" Every year, until the stroke that paralyzed his tongue, restricting him to excited snapping noises, Felder's dad had come up with a new angle on his Colgate gag. After he died, Felder had tried to cook up a few holiday toothpaste jokes of his own, in the old man's honor, but it wasn't the same.)

Even in their office-sweetheart days, Gene had never really fallen into what the manuals they consulted called the Ardent category, sexual relations-wise. She was a long, languid girl who tended to clear her throat after a while and ask if Felder was finished yet. Now, though, all he had to do was stroke her back to send her rippling through a series of shrieks and twitches. Which was fine with Felder—except that twice in one week, he thought he'd heard her pronounce the name Elroy before launching into a bout of twitching shrieks in bed beneath him. This was another new thing he didn't quite get.

Felder had fallen in love with his wife because of her overbite. He was a cream puff for overbites. The sight of one on a languid redhead with a swath of freckles and perfect, mile-long legs had made him swoon the minute he met her. Gene was the only girl he had interviewed to be his dental assistant. He saw her first and simply told the others to go away. As it happened, though, the girl's good looks were not matched by a flair for oral hygiene. Gene would often gaze across a patient's upturned face and hold her nose, her way of hinting that the breath of that peppy bachelor beneath them was "worse than the city dump" (her favorite saying). She talked right over people or commented on their clothes. To her, they were just thirty-two teeth she had to rinse and pick at.

For weeks, Felder wrestled with himself. Finally, he decided he had to either fire her or ask her to marry him. So he did both. Soon thereafter, Mrs. Felder was pregnant with Shecky-Chuck, and Felder had put another ad in *Dental Week*. This time, he hired Uni, a gentle Japanese hygienist with long black hair and such skilled hands that everybody whose plaque she removed came away glowing. Once, over coffee, the petite assistant confided that in Japan, her mother actually got up early to put the toothpaste on her husband's brush. Felder hated to admit it, but he might have liked that—if not every day, then at least on his birthday and major holidays. Instead, for the past eleven years, he'd had Gene, who had announced just last week, their first night in the split-level Felder had nailed down with a variable mortgage—another new thing—that she had no more intention of sitting home watching soaps than she did of hopping to Miami on her clit. That was the kind of remark Gene made lately, which was also sort of new. When Felder met her, she couldn't say "dog doo" without blushing.

"I have my Tupperware, I have my child, I have my shopping, and I have you," Gene informed him. And Felder's heart sank to think that if his wife were an

Olympic event, he wouldn't even have brought home a bronze.

There were new developments at the office, too—such as Mrs. Pfennig's mouth. Mrs. Pfennig was one of dozens of ancient patients Felder had inherited from Dr. Nance, the dentist with whom he'd recently signed on. Nearly all of Nance's patients were of rest-home age. This meant a busload of denture work—never Felder's favorite activity. And yet, in a piece of good fortune that still astonished him, Nance had dropped the entire practice into his lap after state dental inspectors began sniffing around for Medicare infractions. His partner of only a few months, the senior dentist retired at forty-two to concentrate on sport fishing in Bimini. And Felder, invariably, was left with a battery of lucrative blue hairs all his own. Almost without trying, it seemed, he had become fairly wealthy. There were drawbacks, of course—aside from all those retirees, he never got used to showing up every day at a shopping mall, where Nance's office was wedged between The Puff Hut, "a feline boutique," and Mister Jackie's, a hairpiece salon for men. But still, as his wife kept telling him, only a fool would complain about falling into something so sweet. So Felder kept his senior-shopping-mall queasiness to himself.

Mrs. Pfennig, though, was a majestic, well-coifed woman, the widow of a judge. She had a swanlike neck that required his keeping the dental chair as low to the floor as possible. For rear-molar work, Felder, even at

5'8", had to stand on a telephone book. And in recent weeks, Mrs. Pfennig had required massive amounts of rear molar. She'd been in almost constantly, complaining that some fillings Felder had given her were bringing in a country-and-western radio station. What seemed to bother the stately patient was not that her fillings picked up music but the kind of music they were picking up. "Really," she complained, as though this lapse in taste were somehow a reflection on Felder, "they keep playing this dreadful song about Jesus kicking some man's soul through the goal posts of heaven. *Now, that's when Prue Pfennig says enough!*"

As she explained it, all the distinguished old woman wanted was for Felder to tune her in to "some nice Mantovani." And, to his own surprise, Felder found himself canceling other patients, clearing the decks to spend entire afternoons adjusting her fillings, rearranging things, splattering silver compound around on her dentures in hopes of providing the judicial widow some easy listening in her sunset years. For a while, all he could get her was the dispatcher for a taxicab company, followed by a few days of news and weather, and then a batch of staticky police bulletins that Mrs. Pfennig claimed made the roof of her mouth itch.

Most remarkable of all for Felder was not just that he was going along with the music-loving dowager but how much he looked forward to tinkering with her transistorized teeth. It was strange. In the face of his son Shecky-Chuck's request, his wife's unbidden lust, and the general pall of existence as an old people's dentist, the afternoon Mrs. Pfennig leaped up to exclaim that he'd finally snagged her some light classical, it struck Felder as a red-letter day, the high point of his recent life. Not a happy thought. After that, it was back to the other seniors and their crumbling gums.

It might have been this last realization that inspired Felder to walk past his Buick Regal in the mall parking lot that afternoon and just keep walking. Clad in his standard officewear—double-knit flares, brown Hush Puppies, a doctor's smock with three tiny mirrors, and a canine pick still peeking out of the breast pocket—he strolled the two miles from the shopping mall to the interstate, where he stuck out his thumb.

In his wallet that day, Felder held $43, plus some credit cards and an ID from the American Dental Association. "What else?" he asked himself, as a van full of teens slowed down to point at him, "does a guy need to run away from home?"

"You a beautician?" asked the girl behind the wheel after Felder managed to clamber across the gravel shoulder. The van had made an illegal U-turn to pass him twice, which had him a little worried. But when they swung back a third time, he saw it was just a teenaged girl with her younger sister and pesky little brother in back.

"Oh, the smock," said Felder as he climbed aboard. "I'm no beautician." And without thinking, he added, "I'm with the carnival."

The girl driving giggled, but her sister piped right up, "With those duds? You look like a *dentist* to me!"

"Well," said Felder, smoothing the part in his hair and settling in.

The younger sister was a squat girl with a thick face and a short bowl haircut who had popped out of the front seat as soon as Felder scrambled in. She might have been twelve, and resembled a stunted version of the driver, a slender Audrey Hepburn look-alike of seventeen or eighteen. Felder couldn't tell. On the driver, that bowl haircut seemed very stylish, and he imagined it might have been the latest rage in Paris or New York. Gene was always dragging *Vogue*s into bed, but Felder never glanced at them unless she made him read the horoscope page, so she could wait until he was through and remind him that if she'd known about astrology before he proposed, she would never have said yes to a man with Felder's moons.

But now it was the little brother who turned on him. "There ain't no carnival," he croaked, bursting Felder's *Vogue* reverie. The child sounded like Froggy in *The Little Rascals*, and Felder wondered if he was doing it on purpose or if he'd suffered some kind of damage to his glottis. "There ain't no carnival, for one thing," the boy rushed on, "and for another, I know who you are. You're that dentist at the mall. I know, because my grandma went to you once. She said your hands were clammy." The youngster craned his square head over the seat back and put his face right in Felder's, like someone baiting an umpire. "Plus," he said, "I know because you're Shecky-Chuck's dad and he's in my gym class. How come you let him change his name to Shecky, anyway? If I asked my dad something like that, he'd strain my milk!"

"Cool it, Dooley!" the thick sister sniped at him. She rapped the child's bony skull with a metal ruler, and the high-strung Hepburn girl slapped the wheel and laughed. Watching the older sister, Felder forgot his uneasiness over being spotted long enough to think how much he liked her smile. She had the kind of uppers his professor called "perfs," like the ones in the after halves of all the before-and-after charts they studied that semester. The truth was, Felder loved braces. He loved the molding and measuring, loved laying them in. But mostly he loved that little Michelangelo feeling a dentist got when he pried the wires off a once-buck-toothed ten-year-old, then got to watch as the grateful pup finally realized that all the teasing, all the tears and pillow pounding, was worth while. "*No more Bugs Bunny, Mommy!*" It made him sigh.

One of the biggest regrets about his all-senior roster was that few, if any, of your elderlies went in for braces. "Welcome to *Planet of the Dentures*," Nance had toasted him his first day on the job.

"So what *are* you?" the sister in back demanded after hurting her brother. For a second, they stopped bickering, and Felder felt their outraged stares. The driver, he saw, was biting her fist to check her giggles, and Felder had one second where he imagined Gene speeding by on her way to a Tupperware rally, glancing up to see Felder side by side with this lovely but skittish Hepburn child. This seemed like the first whole thought he'd had since his Mrs. Pfennig triumph. He realized all at once that he'd have to make friends with these three or one of them would blab all over school that they'd picked up Shecky-Chuck's dad hitchhiking, *"and he said he was joining the carnival!"* No doubt that bit of news would shame his son, who always seemed slightly ashamed to begin with. Worse, it would be sure to send Gene off to the authorities to haul him back home. Back to the boy's name change and plumbing collection, back to his wife's clit remarks and late-night Elroy noises.

Felder slid inches lower in his seat. "You're part right," he said, trying to chuckle and pat the lad's squarish head. "I *am* a dentist. But I'm also with the carnival. I fill the fat lady's cavities. I'm Stretch Felder, carnival dentist," he said solemnly, only to have the gravel-voiced youth roll his eyes. "Scout's honor!" A Scout pledge always worked with Shecky-Chuck, who wasn't even a Scout, and Felder had hoped it might pass muster here. "Anyway," he went on, "it's my twin brother who treated your grandma. We're both dentists, see, and sometimes I have to hitch in and see him when I need new tools. Like these," he said, seized by sudden inspiration. "Take one!" He plucked a dime-sized molar mirror from his pocket and held it out. "I picked up some extras, so why don't you keep this as a present. Just to keep everything sort of secret."

"Why?" asked the boy. "What did you do?"

"Yeah, what?" His wide-faced sister glared at him.

"*I* didn't do anything," Felder replied. He tried to act casual, though children made him nervous. He didn't know why they were so mean. He was half ready to just throw open the door and risk a major concussion leaping out. He seemed to remember a special on stuntmen that said that if you kept rolling, you couldn't get hurt. Once on his feet, he could dust off and run away all over again. He would count this as a false start. Maybe the next time, he'd get scooped up by some hearty truck driver who'd take him north, get him work in a logging camp. They probably lost a lot of teeth in logging camps, and he could put them back in again. Felder pictured himself in a plaid shirt, bonding the crowns on a jolly red-haired fellow named Corky after a timber mishap. *Doc Felder*, he thought, *Logging Camp Dentist*.

Felder had his fingers wrapped around the door latch, ready to bounce off for the Great Northwest, when the pretty driver pinched him—just reached over and squeezed the love handle that spilled over his slacks. "Hey," she said, smiling her Audrey Hepburn smile. "I don't mind if you fool with Dooley and Isabelle. They're babies. But I know you're a beautician. Soon as I drop them off at Fred's, we'll shoot over to the Barb, maybe do some makeovers."

"Who's Fred?" Felder asked, though he really wanted to know who Barb was.

The girl gave him another smile. "Our father, silly. He gets us the second half of the week. But he works nights, so the minute I drop these two off, I'm heading straight for the Barb. I already decided."

She finished up with a teeny-nose wrinkle that left Felder's mouth dry. He hadn't planned on anything like this when he decided to run away. He hadn't really decided, if you wanted to get technical. He had just sort of waved goodbye to Uni and sauntered off to the mall parking lot—as simple as that. Now that the pretty teenager at the wheel turned out to be so friendly— actually seemed to *like* him—it occurred to Felder that the best part of running away might not be escaping Gene and her Elroy twitches. It might be replacing her with a girl who twitched for *him*—though it was still hard to believe he could inspire anyone who looked ten minutes out of high school to anything like that.

After a half hour of sitting in the van in Fred's driveway, Felder wondered vaguely if he could be arrested for something. Could they just come over and book him for not going home? He had nearly persuaded himself to make a run for it, when the Audrey

Hepburn girl dashed out of the front door and ran across the tiny yard to leap into Felder's side of the van. "Shove over," she cried, tossing the keys into his lap. "Let's go!"

Before Felder even had time to panic, she was banging him on the thigh. "For God's sake, drive!" she shrieked. *"Come on!"* Normally, Felder would have explained that he never drove anything but Buicks, that he didn't know about stick shifts. But there wasn't time. He found the ignition and managed to back down to the street just as a bald man in Bermuda shorts came bursting out of the house. The man was waving something in his hand, and Felder looked away before he could see if it was a gun or not.

*"I should have told you!"* The girl shouted over whatever the bald man was screaming and the crash of a garbage can Felder had sideswiped. *"I'm running away from home!"*

"You . . . *what?"* The garbage can seemed to clatter after them, and Felder had to shout back as they lurched down the street. "Is that why he's mad?"

"N-O spells *no!"* said the girl, tugging the giant T-shirt she wore down over her fishnet stockings. "He's mad 'cause he thinks we eloped. He thinks we're taking his van and going to Vegas."

The girl began to giggle again, and Felder clutched his stomach. Why hadn't he heard how maniacal she sounded before this? With Dooley and Isabelle, the teenager had seemed a textbook big sis. Now Felder peered over and saw a juvenile delinquent, a girl in fishnets. Even her bowl haircut looked antisocial. She still had that Hepburn thing, but Felder realized that for the thousandth time, he'd been taken in by nice teeth.

"We gotta make time," the girl cried, reaching over to punch him in his thigh again. No girl had ever done that before, and he wasn't sure he liked it.

"I don't even know your name," Felder told the girl suddenly, "and I don't know about any Vegas, either. I just want to get out right where I got in."

"It's Evie, and you can't," she said.

"Why can't I?"

"Because," giggled Evie, punctuating each word with a light tap at Felder's groin. "Fred's seen you! He's probably told everybody down at the station what happened. They might even be looking!"

The groin taps got to him, and he felt his resolve weakening. "What station?" he asked, hoping she'd say Exxon or Texaco.

"The TV station, silly. Fred does nightly news briefs on nine—eight-ten, ten-ten, twelve-ten and sign-off, plus bulletins."

"Great," said Felder, though, oddly, now that he had a new reason to run away, he felt better about the whole thing. "Do you really think he saw me?"

"Who cares? We're going straight to the Barb, anyway. You can give yourself a whole new look while you're there."

"But the police!" Felder's palms went clammy, the way they did in deceased denture operations. Looking to stretch their dental dollar, a spate of patients had taken to willing their bridge work to loved ones, like shares in IBM. Whenever Felder had to pluck out a deceased's dentures, his palms became clammy right away. "They'll be looking for this van," he said, shuddering. "I could be *wanted!*"

"Don't be so weird," Evie grinned and showed her lowers, as though they'd discussed fleeing the police together a zillion times. "I told you where I'm going!"

"Well," said Felder, "all I know is, I've never been wanted before. I've never even *known* anyone who was wanted! In all those fugitive movies, you always see these guys in fedoras hanging around train stations or waiting at the airport. . . ."

"God! We're not taking a train," said the girl. "We're in a Ford Econoline van!"

"Okay, then," Felder countered. "What about the roadblocks? The highway patrol?"

In his own mind, the dentist was not sure how he'd stand up against Brad Crawford on a lonely stretch of interstate. He figured he'd be okay if he could sneak out his canine pick. Otherwise, the burly patrolman would probably cut him to ribbons against the hood of his car.

The girl popped a gumball into her mouth and made a face. "They don't *have* roadblocks anymore; they have helicopters. You don't even have to come if you don't feel like it."

*Dick Felder, San Quentin Dentist.* "What I feel like," he told his new friend, "is lying down in the back. You take the wheel."

"A real man," said the girl, and for the life of him, Felder could not tell whether this was the charming Hepburn side of her or the smart-aleck, delinquent side. Who knew? "There's some sucks back there if you want," she told him as he crawled over the seat, "under the spare-tire cover. Just don't be too big a piggo."

Felder had missed the hippie thing entirely. He'd been swept up in dent and predent at the height of it. Only occasionally would he stare wistfully at the rainbow-colored vans as they passed by the campus on their way to such places as Santa Cruz or Colorado. When there were marches on the dinnertime news, he'd gaze a long time at the banners and the protesters packing the parade. For a spell, Felder had thought of starting a dentists-for-peace brigade, a ragtime battery of future malocclusion men, on the march against Amerikan decay. But he never did. The truth was, Felder had never succumbed to hippiedom or radical politics or strange drugs or any kind of extramarital temptation, because he did not want to get in trouble. He could not say for certain what made him this way, any more than he could say what trouble would be like if he ever slipped up and got in a little. All Felder knew was that until this minute, fleeing with Evie, he had never stared trouble right in the face. If it turned out to be no big deal, he'd have to thank his lucky stars he had found out before he was too old to do anything about it.

Felder sighed and ran his fingers over the red fur pasted to the van's floor and sides. Above him, the cherry fuzz poked out between the mirrored tiles stuck to the ceiling. He gazed up at himself and stared dreamily. *Dick Felder, Dentist on the Run . . .*

"Earth to Felder, Earth to Felder," Evie called over her shoulder. "The suck's right beside you, behind the spare."

Felder caught her glare in the rearview and said, "Okey-doke." He felt around under the tire cover—also furred—and pulled out a Sucrets case with a single wrinkled cigarette inside.

The girl tossed back a plastic lighter with a happy face on it, but Felder barely had time to flick it and take a modest puff before she started snapping her fingers. "Oh, terrif," she chided him. "We've got a real greedy-poo back there, don't we?"

Felder did not realize he had passed out until he heard the helicopter landing on his head. "Whoa . . . *hold on there!*" he shouted, opening one eye to see a razor-thin fellow with half his hair shaved off wielding electric barber shears just above him. The left half of the boy's head dripped dirty yellow ringlets. The right showed blotchy pink, like a diseased lamb.

"Evie says you're a famous beautician," the half-haired fellow said over his buzzing implement. "I wanted, like, to do some stuff on you, so you could see it. I'm kinda new, but I think I do some original stuff."

"*Hold on!*" cried Felder again. He needed at least fifteen minutes of David Hartman to really wake up, and here he'd just tumbled out of a chopper nightmare into a live set of clippers.

"Original stuff," the boy was saying. "A whole new you . . . Evie says you have to change what you look like, since her dad saw you kidnap her. They put all the kidnap guys up in the post office, so I figured you wouldn't mind a change."

Felder could hardly take it all in. In his fog, he had only just realized he was no longer in the van. He rubbed his eyes as Evie appeared and knelt beside him. But before he could say a word, she gave him her Audrey look and leaned over to paste her lips on his, releasing a cloud of perfumy smoke inside his mouth. Herpes, he thought automatically, the dentist's enemy! The kiss tickled a spot on his spine he'd never felt before, but the perfumy mouthful sent him straight from sleep into confusion. Chanel brain.

Suddenly, the girl grabbed him by the shoulders and screeched in his face, "All-points bulletin! Fred worked you into his briefs! Eight-ten and ten-ten. Stay tuned!"

"He what? *When?*"

"He tattled," the half-haired youngster interrupted. "That means I get a chance to work on my technique— and you get a new look. One beauty guy helping another."

Evie giggled her way into a nasty cackle, and Felder felt himself flush. "I don't see what's so funny," he said, wishing he could open a vent in his skull and let out some perfume. "I'm supposed to be running away; meanwhile, I'm stuck someplace I don't even know."

"Lighten up," said the girl. "You're at the Barb's."

"*Where is she?*"

Evie rolled her eyes like her baby brother. "There's no she, boob face. It's B-A-R-B, the Be Aware Runaway Brigade. There're twenty-six branches, and the founder's an ex-prostitute. I saw all about it on *Donahue* and called the toll-free number. You're allowed to stay until you decide what you want to do."

"You mean, it's a crash pad?" Felder almost felt like crying.

"A *what?*"

Evie and the half-haired boy exchanged smirks, but Felder didn't notice. "Never mind," he mumbled, as a wave of nostalgia came crashing over him. There was a phase in his life when it seemed as if all the people he knew were either hitching across Europe or "just back from the Coast." From what Felder could gather, they all got to stay in crash pads, bouncing in and out of sleeping bags with girls named Wheat or Zinnia who thought sex was just another plane of existence. Felder, of course, was either off at school or at home tending his summer paper route while they were crashing. (He kept the route until he was twenty-four, when one of the neighbors complained that his eight-year-old ought to have a crack at it.) Frequently, back then, Felder imagined what it would be like in a real crash pad. And now, in his mid-thirties, the owner of a Buick Regal, he had finally landed in one.

Felder felt a little tingly as he gazed around. Things were almost exactly as he had expected. The room in which he was sprawled was bright yellow, as casual as a dorm rec room. In one corner, giant slabs of foam rubber were stacked between a pair of battered couches, and a circle of folding chairs had been set up in the middle. A plastic AM radio blasted next to one of the couches, where a pair of wayward BARBies sat tapping their boots to a tune Felder recognized from Mrs. Pfennig's teeth.

"Listen, guy," said the half-hair, giving Felder's chin a playful punch. "Me and Evie got some important beauty biz. See you back at group, huh?"

"Sure thing," said Felder, too busy soaking it all in to notice as they ambled off.

By now, a handful of young people had come straggling in, the new kind he recognized as punks. Not *punk* punks, like when he was in high school—guys with pointy shoes who smoked Pall Malls in the boys' room—but modern punks, with spiky hair and earrings and swastikas on their jackets. Felder had read about them in *Time*.

As Felder basked in his crash-pad experience, a swollen-looking youth swaggered over and stuck out his hand. The boy was clad entirely in denim, with gaping holes at both knees and a red bandanna around his ankle. One of his front teeth was missing, and he wore a peroxide crew cut. Felder was not sure which kind of shake to go with—a standard or the soul shake favored in his own day. As it happened, the swollen, peroxide boy didn't shake at all but just slapped his hand sideways, capping the gesture with a clap on Felder's back. "Bad 'do," said the boy. "I heard you're into doing makeup for videos. I guess that's a good job for dressing any way you want. That's my problem. I could see getting a job and everything, but I can't find one where you can dress the way you want."

"It's a definite plus," Felder said. Not sure whether or not the boy was making fun of him, he checked down at his flares and Hush Puppies. He knew his slacks were "out" but hadn't gotten around to deflaring them yet. Now here he was, running away, stuck with flapping ankles while all these kids were packed into their snug straight-legs.

"Don't worry, it works," said the half-haired boy, as though reading the dentist's fears about his appearance. Felder had not even noticed he was back. He hunched with his ringlet side facing him, winding the cord around his clippers and slipping them into a Greyhound kit bag. "The flares, the Puppies, the hairstyle—it's a special look. It's, like, *really* you. . . ."

"Well, *I* found him," Evie chimed in, and Felder tingled again to think she might actually like him. But then, mooning up at her, he realized something had happened. Since she had gone off with the clippers fellow, her bowl haircut had become a melon slice, a cantaloupe plume sprouting down the middle of a baldy. She'd gone Mohawk.

"We're twins," she giggled at Felder's surprise. "I told Oleo I wanted just what he gave you."

"*Oleo?*" Things weren't sinking in. "That's me," said the budding beautician, raising his Greyhound bag. "Have snips, will Mohawk!"

Felder chuckled right along with them, though he was not sure he understood. A moment later, the door opened and a chill hit his scalp. He reached up and gasped. The side of his head felt like a kneecap. He quickly touched the other side—more kneecap—and was about to cry out when he felt the thick swath of hair left in the middle.

"Thank God!" he sighed. Felder knew he must look pretty peculiar, but just knowing he had that swath, if nothing else, made him feel a bit better.

He stopped touching himself as a tiny pimpled girl ambled over to their group and sat at his feet. The waif arranged a patent-leather hatbox on her lap and began talking. "You're new here, right? Okay, we've got counseling, individual and group, plus a deal with the phone company so kids can call their parents if they decide they want to go home, free of charge. I've got a kitty," she confided, tapping her hatbox, "but house rules are *no pets*, so I only let her out in the laundry room. Her name's Ethel, the same as mine."

"You're a lucky little lady," said Felder. He never knew what to say to strange children—including his own son. But as the room started to fill, more and more rambling teens came to cluster around him, to hang out with a veteran runaway. Evie rested her head on Felder's shoulder. The tiny pimpled girl knelt at his feet and Oleo stood proud sentry beside him. A little hemmed in, Felder tried to rearrange his legs on the floor, going tailor seat. This was when he expected someone to pull out a folk guitar and break into "Michael (Row the Boat Ashore)" while everybody held hands and swayed. Felder had never done any serious swaying and wondered if there might be some on the agenda. But all the adolescents seemed to want to do was chat.

"I guess you've been on the road since *Saturday Night Fever*," ventured the pimpled girl with a kind of awe. And Felder felt a dozen pairs of teenaged eyes just glowing at him.

"I've been around," he said quietly, striking what he hoped was a rugged, world-weary pose for his new fans.

"The guy's even got *Hush Puppies!*" Oleo pointed at Felder's toast-colored loafers and shook his head. "That's class!"

"You work in video," sighed the peroxide boy, "you get to wear what you want."

They went on like that, Felder less than certain how to enjoy his newfound status. He guessed it was already about eleven—somehow he'd lost his graduation watch, inscribed HAPPY TOOTHACHES, FROM DAD— and Felder was anxious to find out when the lights went off. He still wanted to sample some sleeping-bag action, even if everyone else his age had tried it fifteen years before.

"Do we all . . . *sleep* here?" he whispered to Evie, but just then, a strapping fellow of thirty or so strode into the room. "That's Brother Hank," the girl hissed, jamming an elbow into Felder's soft middle. "It's *counseling* time."

"You mean, a rap session?" This was another new experience, and Felder was excited. The counselor looked comfortable in his turtleneck and khakis, like a man who knew how to handle youth groups. He straddled a tall stool up front and raised his right hand for quiet.

"'Evening, boys and girls."

"*Evening, Brother Hank.*"

"Any new faces?"

"Me," Evie piped up, indicating Felder, "and this is the guy who drove me."

Felder gave a sheepish wave, and a very young boy he hadn't seen before stood up and bowed. "Ace, here," said the boy, who might have been in sixth grade. He had on a pair of leather pants, a leather vest, and a half dozen crisscrossing chains.

"Glad to see all of you," said Brother Hank. "Welcome! Now, Ace, how did you happen to join us?"

The boy glanced around the runaway circle, then gave his shoulders a tough little roll. "Daddy's in petrodollars, see? One day, he comes home and starts bawling about the crumbling price structure. He starts drinking martinis. He doesn't stop, see? That's a week ago. Then, this morning, he gives the old lady two black eyes. 'You're next,' he goes. 'You're not leaving this house!' And then—"

"*Hang on!*" Felder had sat through as much of this as he could. "You can't be more than eleven or twelve," he butted in. "I have a son nearly your age. His name used to be Chuck."

Ace clammed up, giving another shoulder roll, and Brother Hank aimed his smile Felder's way. "You are?"

"Dick Felder, DDS," Felder said. The counselor nodded. "What you're saying, doctor, is that you ran away from home and your son stayed?"

"Well," Felder heard himself say, "he likes it there. . . ."

"Maybe you and I should speak later, in my office," said Brother Hank, glaring at him a second before getting back to Ace.

Felder's ears burned bright red. It was like getting yelled at in junior high, except now he was the same age as the teacher. Maybe the BARB wasn't for him. While Brother Hank went on to review kitchen privileges, Felder kept busy trying to make out bits of graffiti.

Everybody broke off in twos and threes after the session, and Felder found himself on the couch with the swollen, peroxide boy. His name turned out to be Link. Felder listened to Link's career-and-wardrobe problems, meanwhile trying to decide whether to talk to Brother Hank or to just walk out. He wasn't sure it would go down in the books as running away, but he thought of calling a cab to whisk him back to the interstate. He'd be blowing his shot at any on-the-floor stuff with Evie, but still. . . .

Without making his mind up one way or the other, Felder leaped to his feet and announced that he was going for a walk. He could not spot Evie anywhere, and on a whim he asked Link if he knew where the freeway was. "Around the corner," sighed the swollen blond. "I guess a guy like you has a lot of cool videos to go back to." He made Felder take his name and his mother's address—in case anything "came up"—and they shook hands.

To Felder's surprise, the freeway really was around the corner. Weirder yet, when he stepped outside, he saw that the runaway house was a duplex on a tree-lined street in a normal residential area. He had expected a minority neighborhood.

A horseshoe drive wound down to the curb, and at the bottom Felder heard a peculiar mewing. It seemed to be coming from a parked Econoline van—little Evie's. He stepped toward it and tapped on the rear door. "What's up?" he called in his professional voice. "You okay?"

There was no answer for a second; then the door fell open and Felder got a blast of stale perfume smoke. "Oh, it's you," Evie mumbled, sounding hoarse and averting her eyes. "Come on in, I guess."

It was dark inside, but as he followed, Felder could see that the girl had nothing on but that giant T-shirt with RELAX across the back. He made his way cautiously, taking stooped, tiny steps until they reached a giant beanbag pillow up by the seats. Evie settled in against the bag and looked away from Felder. "I got the heebie-jeebs," she confessed. "I came out here to think."

"Me, too."

Felder lowered himself and nestled beside her. He couldn't help gaze at the way her perfect high school legs sort of *languished* in front of him, crossed at the ankle, her smooth thighs bare against the scarlet pile. His own luck scared him.

"You're shaking," Felder said, half to take attention from his own quivers, and Evie laughed her brave little *Breakfast at Tiffany's* laugh. "I made a mistake," she whispered, as if it were the saddest secret in the world, and Felder felt something snap in his chest. He wasn't sure whose arms had flown around whom, but next thing he knew, they were rolling in that synthetic fur, Evie's fingers working his Sansabelt while he kissed the tears out of her mascara.

In no time, Felder was sprawled naked on the itchy fiber, Evie beside him, with her T-shirt pushed up to her navel. As they embraced, Felder got a glimpse of their reflection in the mirrored ceiling. He'd always wanted to try it with mirrors—not with Gene, necessarily—but was not sure if this qualified, since he couldn't recognize himself. What thrill was it watching a couple frolic in the mirror if you weren't sure which one was you? Was that him—*in the Mohawk?* For a few seconds, his stomach threatened to quease up. *What would his patients think?* But no sooner did he quease up than he dequeased. He had a *flash*, as they used to say, that there was no point worrying about his haircut. What good had a regular boy's ever done him? He'd had a regular boy's for thirty years and had ended up with a Tupperware wife and a fleet of senior denture wearers. He'd had the Mohawk half a day, and here he was tussling in a mirrored van with a lovely eighteen-year-old.

The thought fortified him, and Felder got back into the swing. The trouble was, he'd never seen his own buttocks before, and every time he looked up, *there they were*. He had no idea how much hip fat he'd been packing on. But somehow, Evie worked it so his bottom was always in view, and Felder had to struggle to forget about it. "Come on," the girl panted in his ear. "Really ride me, Daddy!" As they got going, she kept up the patter like a peppy infielder, squealing, "Make me bad, make me *real* bad!" until Felder asked if she could quiet down for a sec so he could concentrate. He wasn't used to all that chatter, and he had a feeling she'd picked it up from some kind of movie.

The second he'd spoken up, Felder knew he had blown it. Evie stopped wriggling, and her voice went flat. "Don't mind me," she huffed, and Felder found himself more or less finishing up on his own.

The girl maintained a sullen silence until he was through, at which point she said "ooh-ah" and pulled her T-shirt back down.

So now he'd done it. Felder had hitchhiked, had tried sex in a van. He'd been to a crash pad and gotten a wild haircut. He'd even tried drugs. It occurred to him that this pretty much covered all the fun things he could have done if he'd run away years ago—in a single day. If he wanted to, he could just pop back into the office the next morning, a new man.

Felder considered all this as he stood under a street-light, buttoning his smock. The freeway, as Link had promised, was just down the road, and Felder could hardly explain the cheer he felt as he strolled up the on-ramp. He stuck out his thumb as the first head-lights approached. They turned out to be from a Wonder Bread truck, which struck him as wholesome. He could use a little wholesomeness, he thought, after what he'd been through.

Felder took a step forward when the bread truck slowed. He gave a big grin, but the driver only slid open his window and hollered something that sounded like "No Greek"—whatever *that* meant. Still, as chilly as the night was getting, Felder felt stout of spirit. He stamped his feet and clapped his hands together. It started drizzling, which was okay, too, since most folks would probably feel sorry for a lonely soul out on the highway in rainy weather. He knew it was late—he had never found his HAPPY TOOTHACHES watch—but it wasn't *that* late. A half dozen more automobiles went by, nearly all slowing to stare and point, until Felder himself was obliged to turn around and look behind him, just to see what they were gawking at.

At last, as the drizzle turned to a light downpour, a car whooshing off in the distance gave Felder a special feeling. "This one's lucky," he said out loud, blowing into his hands. He held out his thumb with what he felt was a longing gaze. In the old days, all the kids would do up giant signs saying things like CALIFORNIA or WEST! But even if he'd thought of it, Felder knew he would have felt too silly holding up a square of cardboard saying mall.

As the car swung into view, Felder gave a happy yelp. A *Buick!* Since he drove one himself, Felder felt a special affinity for other Buick owners. They weren't as showy as, say, Cadillac owners. They were regular people who made enough money to live comfortably without getting cocky about it—Dick Felder's kind of people.

The Le Sabre approached and slowed down on the shoulder before him.

"How do!" Felder called out and trotted up to lean into the passenger window. He saw to his relief that the man at the wheel was actually Mister Jackie, owner of the hairpiece salon beside him in the mall. "*Mister Jackie*," Felder cried. "It's me, Dick Felder—the dentist next door!"

The wig man stared for a second, and the window shot back up. Felder saw his reflection in the window. For the second time, it startled him. He looked like a middle-aged Apache. The gleaming sides of his skull lent the rest of his face a leering, demented sheen.

The toupee baron sped off and left him in a spray of gravel. "Wait!" Felder yelled. "*I've got an office. . . .*"

He kept on that way, yelling and chasing after the car, long after it had disappeared down the highway. By now it was pouring, and Felder had no choice but to keep on running.

# L'IL DICKENS

I did not mean to sodomize Dick Cheney.

I mean, I'm not even gay. Or not usually. But when, to my surprise, I bumped into him—literally—at the counter of Heimler's Guns and Ammo, in Caspar, something clicked. And I'm not talking about the safety on my Mauser.

You see, there's another side to "L'il Dickens," as the vice-president liked to refer to himself. Or, at least, a certain part of himself. *En privato,* he's tender. He's funny. He's pink. And he's a gun man, just like me.

But there I go, getting ahead of myself. . . . See, I was in Wyoming to pick up some German pistols. Not, you know, that I'm some kind of Nazi gun freak. Not even close. I just like the workmanship. The craft. A taste, as it happens, shared by Mister Cheney.

"Schnellfeuer Pistole," he smiled, eyes aglow as he surveyed my weapon.

"Model 1912," I smiled back. "Recoil, single action."

"May I?"

He held out his hand. I had yet to recognize him. In his black-and-red hunting cap, flaps down, he could have been any pudgy hunter. Some sneering Elmer Fudd. But his nails were beautiful. Buffed as a show-room Bentley. I slapped the gun in his palm, butt first. "Good heft." His lips parted—fleshy magenta outside, meat-red within. "What are we looking at, ten inches?" "Eleven."

The VP licked his lips and let out a trademark grunt. "Mmm . . . barrel?"

"Five-and-a-quarter."

"Pocket-size. Nice."

"Looks can be deceiving." Our eyes met through his bifocals and I felt a shiver. "Short bolt travel makes the rate of fire astronomical. But there's no control."

My new friend gave a little laugh that sounded like *hug-hug-hug*. "Believe it or not, I lose control myself."

*"Really?"*

Suddenly I had feelings I couldn't name. We'd drifted to the back of the store—no more than a counter, really, flanked by locked rows of weapons on the wall and a signed photo of George Bush Junior in his flight suit, helmet under his arm, eyes triumphant, basket padded. His Mission Accomplished moment.

At some point the owner, a scruffy fellow who looked like Wilfred Brimley, had slung a BACK-IN-TEN sign in the window and disappeared. Maybe my future love mate had given him a signal.

"Gee," I heard myself say, "you look a lot like—"

"I am," he said, "but you can call me . . . L'il Dickens."

He held open a door to the back room, which turned out to be more than that. Even as my eyes took it in: sturdy mahogany desk and chairs, the portrait of J. Edgar Hoover over the crackling fire, the shelves stacked with sheaves of documents, busts of Lincoln, Jefferson, and Julius Caesar and finally, as my eyes adjusted to the dark, the single bed in the corner. Rough green blanket tucked sharply under the mattress in military corners.

"Spartan," he growled. "A man in my position can't afford to be soft. We are, after all, at war."

"Wait? Is this the bunker?"

"Negative. The Veepeock is technically in the White House basement. Everybody knows it. That's the problem."

"Veepeock. I'm not sure I—"

"VPEOC. White House terminology. Short for Vice Presidential Emergency Operations Center." He cut me off, clearly a fellow used to getting his way. "You didn't think the bunker was in Washington, did you? That place is a cesspool of acronyms."

"But shouldn't there be security? Surveillance? Cameras?"

"Sometimes you don't want anybody looking. *Hug-hug-hug.*" He tapped the cot. "Come on over here, soldier."

"Okay." Jesus!

In spite of myself, I drifted toward him. The man had tremendous animal magnetism. A musky aura of power seemed to emanate from his scalp. But still . . . shouldn't there be pull-down wall maps? Advisors? Data banks? A red phone with a key in it: hotline to Moscow . . . or Baghdad? Or Crawford?

I had, I realized, conflated Cheney's love nest with the president's war room in *Dr. Strangelove.* But I wasn't hobnobbing with Peter Sellers. Instead, here I was, rubbing cheek to grizzled cheek with the real vice president, arguably the most powerful man in the free world. Freakish but true. While I stood there, frozen with fear, he looked up and licked my face.

"Did you just *lick* me?"

My breath, as they say, came in short pants. Cheney chuckled, ignoring my question, and swept his arm before him, indicating his little patch of heaven.

"I like a barracks feel. . . . It's more . . . *manly.*"

"But you didn't actually serve, did you? What was it, five deferments? You dropped out of Yale, then went to community college because of the draft. I heard your wife even had a baby nine months to the day after they ended the childless married deferments."

His face reddened. A tiny wormlet of vein began to throb at his left temple. For one bad moment I thought he was either going to kill me or stroke out on the spot. Instead, he began to hug-chuckle all over again. "That Lynne. Bent her over the sink and slipped her the

Dickens. Out came L'il Mary, right on time. My daughter's good people. Even if she is gay as Tallulah Bankhead's fanny."

With that he gave me another smooch. I wanted to recoil. And yet . . . I couldn't fight it. There was no other way. I had to ask. "Are you gay, Mister Vice President?"

"Me?" He leapt from the cot and ripped off his flannel with such ferocity I feared he might tear a ligament. "I had so many chicks in high school they used to call them Cheney-acs."

Before this, I admit, I never knew the meaning of the word *swoon*. I couldn't help but stare at his tufted belly roll, his hairless chest and—be still my heart—his pacemaker. Yes and yes again!

Embedded under the skin over his left nipple was the outline of what looked like a pack of Luckies. He saw me ogling and beckoned. "Wanna touch?"

I nodded.

"Figured you might."

Slowly, I raised my fingers to his subcutaneous square. "It's . . . it's so *hard*."

What can I say? He was overweight, and grunting, and no doubt capable of having me disappeared with a single phone call. But God he was sexy. Soon my tentative touches turned to stroking, my stroking to outright caresses. Our eyes locked. The veep parted his meaty lips.

With that, it was on. Lynne's hubby yanked off his belt, let his pants drop around the tops of his waders, and popped his thumbs under the elastic of his white undies, which rode so high on his belly, they covered the button. "Big girl panties!"

Then he turned, waggling his ample bottom, and dropped to his hands and knees beside the army cot. I wasn't sure how to react, but before I could, he grunted, stretched, and pulled out a monkey-head bong.

"Who does this remind you of?"

It's all a little foggy after that. Yes, he reached in my pants and chuckled that he'd found the weapon of mass destruction. Yes, he wanted me to duct tape the cheeks of his buttocks. Yes he wanted me to spank and penetrate him and call his organ "L'il Dickens." The problem is, I've never really been that into grass. It always hits me harder than anybody else. And there are blank spots, which is just as well, since, even now, my gorge rises at the very notion of anal sex with an aging fat man who voted against Martin Luther King Day.

After our "encounter," he rolled off and, to my surprise, began to recite, in that trademark Oval Office–adjacent growl, albeit a tad slurry after the high-grade government kush:

*I saw the best minds of my generation destroyed by madness, starving hysterical naked,*

*dragging themselves through the negro streets at dawn, looking for an angry fix.*

After meeting the vice president, touching his pace-maker, and pounding him with a savagery that still makes me cringe, I did not think anything could surprise me. But hearing him recite *Howl* did just that. His passion was palpable. Or so it seemed. . . . Maybe he was just trying to impress me. When I glanced over, he snarled from the side of his mouth. "Ginsberg was a bottom, too. . . . *Hug-hug-hug.*"

After that I passed out. I may have been behind the gun store for twenty minutes or an entire day. When I came to, he was fully dressed and clutching a shotgun.

"You know I have to kill you," he said.

It was hard to tell if he was serious. You think Cheney, you don't think joke. But the shotgun in his hand was not smiling. "Remember Harry?"

"Harry Whittington? The guy you accidentally shot in the face? When you were quail hunting?"

By way of response, he thrust the muzzle toward my face and yelped. "BLAMMO!" It was the first time I saw him smile. And I quickly wished he'd stop. That rictus grin was scarier than his persistent scowl.

"Quail's a front," he said, looming over me.

Here—finally—was the proverbial Dark Force of legend. He raised his shotgun and racked it.

"There was no hunting accident," he went on, talking out of the side of his mouth. "I heard Harry was two-timing me. That bastard."

"You mean it was a lover's spat?"

"I shot him in the face." He sneered his trademark sneer. "But I was aiming for his huevos."

So saying, he stared off. That double barrel was still pointed my way. But my lover seemed to have withdrawn into himself. Indeed, to my amazement, he wiped away a tear. This was my chance.

I began to back away. One step, two . . . three. I felt behind me for the door. My fingers grazed the knob. Got it! But, just as I prepared to make my escape, Dick Cheney lowered the gun, turned away and, as if pulled by invisible heartstrings, moved to a closed door. Sighing audibly, he opened it. A closet. Over his shoulder I could see within, where a single flannel shirt hung on a hanger. "Harry . . . Harry . . . Harry," he said, burying his face in the buckshot-riddled flannel.

I knew I should leave, but I was touched. We'd shared something, after all. Tenderly, L'il Dickens rubbed the holey material against his face. Tenderly, he inhaled the must of lost desire. Here it was. Brokeback Neo-Con. I felt myself tearing up, though at the same time I was concerned about the nagging chafe on my scrotum.

For another beat, I lingered. And then, I left him. The vice president the rest of the nation would never see. The burly, pink-thighed, sneering buffalo of love. I'll never forget you, Dick. Though, God knows, I've been trying.

# FINNEGAN'S WAIKIKI

Finnegan was halfway through *Family Feud* when he got the update on his dad's prostate.

"Harry, phone!" his wife yelled down from their bedroom, where she was packing shoes for her tropical vacation. They had agreed on separate trips this year, at the urging of Dr. Fern, their marriage counselor, though Finnegan was still not sure how he felt about Marge's toddling off to Bora Bora unescorted. "Harry, it's your father's *thing* again. It's flared up. . . ."

"All right," Finnegan called from the rec room. "I'll take it on the princess."

For a second more, he stayed where he was, while Richard Dawson planted wet kisses on a jumbo Montana woman, mother of six. The man would put his tongue anywhere. But why? Finnegan got up and flicked off the set with a heavy sigh. Lately, news of his dad's condition sent waves of dread sweeping over him, leaving him moist and weak-kneed. It was as though once the old man landed terminal gland trouble, it would be only a matter of time till he passed on and left it to his only son, like shares in Monsanto.

"Pop, it's me," Finnegan shouted when he grabbed the kitchen phone. "How's the boy?"

"This isn't your pop," said a girl at the other end, "and you don't have to talk so loud. The phone company does wonderful things with satellites."

"Oh . . . Bambi," said Finnegan, and he settled in against the dishwasher. Bambi was the perky twenty-four-year-old his father had wed after Finnegan's mom had lost her bout with lupus. For two-and-a-half years, the old man had nursed her, never complaining, doing all the things a loyal, loving husband would do. And two weeks after she went into the ground, he snapped up Bambi and moved to Waikiki, where he lived in some kind of rest home with a bunch of people he referred to as "swingers." *Hey, kiddo, come on down!* he'd holler in his weekly calls—an ex-gossip columnist, Finnegan Sr. was used to hollering on phones to make himself heard over jumping city desks, a habit his son had inherited—*Come on down and see the swingers! Have some fun for a change!* But so far, Harry had bowed out. He had not even met his stepmother face-to-face. He'd only seen her in the snapshots the old guy was always mailing along. Ten years younger than Harry, Bambi looked a little like Morgan Fairchild and struck Finnegan as the sort of girl who popped out of cakes. In fact, that's how the old guy had met her, when she leaped out of an eight-layer at a reunion of his dad's old magazine, *Uncensored*. After leaving newspapers, his pop had gone on to write for the "glossies," as he always called them, popping along from *Confidential* to *SIN-sensational*, on up the ladder to *Uncensored* before the market dried and he retired to stay home and care for Finnegan's mother.

What bothered Harry, he supposed, was that Bambi was so much better looking than his own wife, a horsy brunette who seemed to have lost her waistline sometime around 1975.

"So how is he?" Harry asked before Bambi could launch into another subject. If you didn't steer her, he'd discovered, the girl would just sort of ramble on until you either had to put the phone down or tell her the surrounding five-block area was engulfed in flames. "Marge tells me he's had a flare-up . . ."

"Well, gee," Bambi sighed, the first time he'd ever heard her less than vivacious. "It's kinda worse than that. They were gonna operate, then they weren't. And now he's got the emphysema, *plus* cancer of the thingy, so they had to go in and put a little tent up over the waterbed. It's, like, this giant gator bag, and Bernie was all upset 'cause he wanted to keep his Sony portable in there with him. You know how he loves *Hawaii Five-O*. But like I keep telling him, 'Bernie, you're already in Hawaii, so—'"

"Bambi, please," Finnegan cut in, "just tell me what's going on."

There was quiet for a second; then Finnegan heard a sniffle. "I think you ought to come down, Harry. He asked special."

"That bad, huh?"

Finnegan was already making calculations. He wondered if this would count as his vacation—going to see his dad in an Oahu oxygen tent.

"All right. I'll catch the next plane out." He spoke as gently as possible, half surprised by the girl's concern. This was an all-new Bambi, or else he'd had her wrong all along. "Just don't worry, okay? The old guy's always been lucky."

"Let's hope," Bambi blubbered, "but you better *wiki wiki*."

"I don't know if that's legal," said Harry, happy to hear a giggle at the other end.

"You *silly*, that means 'hurry up.' I'm scared to death."

"On my way," he promised, and he felt a lot better when they hung up. So what if it did count the same as Marge's stint in the South Pacific? He had to be there, and he would.

Finnegan felt almost noble as he trooped up the stairs to give his wife the news. "Honey," he announced, catching her bent over before the mirror, trying on Bermudas—not his favorite view—"you may have to find another ride to the airport tomorrow night; Dad needs me in Waikiki right away."

"He . . . what?" Marge met his eyes in the full-length. "Is it awful?"

"Bambi says *wiki wiki*," he said gravely, leaving her tugging at a zipper while he skipped back down to the princess to make his reservations.

Harry himself had no idea why he felt so giddy.

From the second Bambi met Finnegan Jr. at the airport, she had been eager to tell him how well his father looked, how smoothly all his bodily functions still operated, as though the old man were some kind of farm implement Harry had come all this way to consider purchasing. "It's amazing," she bubbled, leading her legal stepson into the bungalow and up to the tent beneath which her husband appeared to be sleeping peacefully.

In the dusk, Finnegan Sr. did appear remarkably well, if a tad pallid. He still sported a full head of hair, which he slicked straight back and kept a shimmering black with daily applications of Skuff Kote. As far back as Harry could remember, he'd been dousing his waves with the old-fashioned olive brush that came with the polish. When the Skuff Kote folks switched over to a modern sponge applicator, Harry's dad stocked up on the original bottles, and one of the young Finnegan's fondest father-son recollections was of watching his pop dip in the tiny brush, then daintily swab on shoe polish, taking special care with his natty, Ameche-like mustache.

The old man lay flat on his back, like he always had, his hands behind his head and his legs crossed at the ankle. He was the only person Harry knew who slept with his legs crossed, as though in a deck chair.

"You're right; he looks fantastic," Harry whispered, though something was still a little off. It was so obvious, it took a few seconds to see what it was. "*Why the hell doesn't he have any clothes on?*"

"Oh, Harry," chuckled the perky blonde. "You're just like him."

"What?"

"Come on, you nut," said the girl. "We'll have plenty of time to kid around tomorrow. Right now, I'm going to change, then we've got to get you to your bungalow. We had to put you in Honeymoonland, 'cause just about everything's booked up. I wanted to slide you right in here with us, but your daddy said three's a crowd."

Bambi seemed one hundred percent more chipper now than she had on the phone. She did not show the least discomfort standing in front of the nude old man, and Harry had a feeling it could have been anyone— his father, Marvin Hamlisch, or Ted Koppel—and it would not have made a lick of difference to her if he was naked. He realized as they turned to leave that, except for a simple terry robe that barely covered her own bottom, she was just about in the buff herself. She was tinier than he had imagined but still very much in the Fairchild mold.

When she saw him gawking, Bambi pranced back and gave him a peck on the chin. "I know what you're wondering—why the hoopy-doop does she have a robe on? Well, the one thing about going *au naturel* is the buggy bites. Especially at night. They don't seem to bother you-know-who. But they like me, so that's why I sometimes slip into this old thing. To protect the investment, as Bernie says."

"That's not what I was thinking," Harry said, but Bambi wasn't listening. The girl had already grabbed his hand and was tugging him out of his dad's quarters back into the courtyard. From what Harry could tell, Waikiki Haven consisted of clusters of round, overgrown cabanas, separated by palm trees and winding paths that led to other cabanas and more palms. The beach was nowhere to be seen, but they passed a pair of kidney-shaped pools—one just for "waders," Bambi explained with a little nose wrinkle—as well as a blossom-covered gazebo, a horseshoe pit, shuffleboard courts, and a long, low building Harry guessed had to be for dining. Strings of colored lights sagged between the bungalows, lending the tropical rest home a makeshift, carnival feeling, like a summer camp fixed up for parents' weekend. To Finnegan, the air smelled like Glade.

"You missed the luau," said his jaunty stepmother, walking him by a fenced-in barbecue pit where a few cinders still sizzled in the dark.

"Story of my life," said Harry. "But what I still don't get is why you and Dad are the only people I've seen. It's only eight and the place is deserted."

"Bingo night," Bambi giggled and gave his hand a squeeze. "They bus 'em out at six and bus 'em back in again around eleven. The only kids who skip bingo are the 'mooners,'" she whispered, leading him down a dirt path between smaller cabanas with their names on little stilts out front. They passed Deep Dish Apple and Baked Alaska, where plaintive cries of "Herbie, Herbie!" leaked out into the night. Bambi continued to speak in hushed tones, as though they'd entered a hospital zone. "They named all the bunks in Honeymoonland after desserts. I think that's kind of cute."

"Me, too," said Harry, going *sotto voce* himself, not wanting to spoil the mood. "Which one am I in?"

"Spicecake," Bambi said, smiling, and she gave his fingers another squeeze. "The same as your dad and me our first night."

There was nothing Finnegan could think of to say to this. He simply trailed behind in silence as the girl skipped up the three steps to the honeymoon suite, trying not to stare at the perfect handfuls her teeny robe revealed as she took each one.

"For God's sake, she's your mother," he said to himself, causing his hostess to turn around and ask if he'd said something. "Oh, no . . . I mean, just how I'm glad we're related," he said lamely. But Bambi hardly noticed. She was too busy fiddling with the oil lamp, digging Finnegan's blanket out of the bureau drawer and generally making things just so for his visit.

Harry waited by the door in his business suit, doing his best to stay composed while his tempting stepmom puttered about her tasks.

"*Voilà!*" she cried at last, with a little curtsy. And then she bounced backward onto the bed so that her robe flew open and Harry saw everything he'd been struggling not to for the past five minutes. "I'm pooped!" she laughed, lolling back on the mattress, which seemed to buoy her up and sink down into itself before settling. "These water beds are just like curling up in a womb, don't you think?"

"I don't know," said Harry. "I've never been in one."

"You're kidding! Well, Harry Finnegan, *come on down!*"

Bambi giggled and patted a spot beside her. The bed began to undulate, sending the girl up and down again, rising and failing as she lay down, exposing every inch of herself to his nervous gaze. It had been so long since Harry had seen a woman, a really gorgeous woman—for better or worse, he could not count the waistless Marge—that he felt his mouth go dry. She had the tiniest belly, the palest hair, the most delicately arching throat. . . . All that, plus champagne-cup breasts that spilled neither right nor left but remained there, the nipples good little soldiers just waiting for a command. Harry sighed, his fingers tightening around the strap of his leather-look bag.

"Your father and I like to play life raft," Bambi said brightly. "We sort of bounce around till things really start to roll; then we pretend we're trapped together on stormy waters. Babes at sea . . ."

"Babes at sea," Harry repeated, his voice going husky.

He had to lean on the doorjamb while the girl who was his father's bride threw her head back and laughed. Nothing in Harry's life had prepared him for such a situation: for being older than his stepmother, to begin with, not to mention finding her bare-skinned on a water bed, exposed from platinum head to rosy toenails, while his prostate-damaged dad lay wheezing in his sleep just five minutes down the road. Some things Emily Post had just never got around to covering.

"Bambi," Finnegan blurted, feeling the blood rush to his face. "Bambi, I just want to—"

"Yes?"

"I just want to say I like you, *as a mother*," he heard himself say.

"And I like *you*," tittered the sumptuous blonde, "my only son. Maybe tomorrow, if Bernie's up to it, we can have a picnic."

"Swell," said Harry. Then, to his mixed relief and disappointment, the diminutive beauty hopped off the bed and rushed over to smooch him on the forehead.

"If I had to have a child," she confided on the way out, "I'm glad it was you."

Again, Finnegan was speechless. He remained in the doorway, watching his young relation sway off into the night. Faint cries of "Herbie! Herbie!" could still be heard wafting out of Baked Alaska, and for a second longer, he gazed up at the stars. He'd have to call Dr. Fern. He'd been there only an hour, and he already had a whole new batch of marital problems he needed to kick around.

The chanting must have begun around seven, but Harry felt as though he'd just dozed off. Something about the water bed, the way it sort of churned when he rolled over, kept him hopping out to stand over the bowl every couple of hours. He wasn't sure if he felt nauseated or if he just wasn't used to the feel of fluid-packed plastic shifting under his vital organs. As the chorus drew closer—it seemed to be marching on his cabana—he dug in, face down, on the percale, clasping the single pillow provided over his head and squishing it against both ears.

"Shall we give it to him?" cried a man with a voice like Jiminy Cricket's.

"You bet!" sang the rest of the gang, and Harry's annoyance turned to panic as they clomped up the steps to his bungalow and began to chant:

"We know what you're *do*-in'! We know what you're *do*-in'!"

They kept it up for what seemed like centuries. Then a tingle in the back of his neck told Harry they were actually staring at him, that if he lifted up the pillow even an inch, he would see them. They'd be there waving and smiling through one of the bungalow portholes.

"C'mon, you newlies! Shake a leg!" It was Jiminy Cricket again. "There's plenty of time for that stuff. We've got some volleyball to play!"

"Go 'way," Finnegan muttered, and he realized they couldn't hear him just mumbling like that into the bedding. Keeping the pillow clamped over his head, he edged his face off the mattress and shouted, "All alone . . . family emergency!" Then he laid his head back down and hoped they'd wander off.

"What'd he say?" came a voice after a few seconds.

"He says he's alone," said another.

"Honeymoon horror! You know what *that* means!" It was the crickety ringleader. "She left him! The bride's gone back to Momma!"

There was a sympathetic hush, during which Finnegan burrowed deeper in the sloshing mattress. He'd just begun to drift back off when a female voice started in again. "We just can't leave the poor bunny! This is when a person really needs some support!"

"She's right," chimed in Jiminy, to a rising tide of *All right!*s and *Go for it!*s. "Okay, fella, come out with your hands up. Or the honeymoon fun squad's comin' in!"

"No," Harry mumbled weakly, *"no!"* He heard his cabana door being opened and wanted to disappear. He hadn't locked it, could not even remember if the thing *had* a lock. It sounded like one hundred fun seekers were piling in, and Harry played desperately at sleep, even though he'd have had to be deaf not to hear the racket.

"Up and at 'em, big guy!"

When Finnegan stayed catatonic, the ringleader leaned down and blew into a referee's whistle. Then he dapped his hands and addressed the group. "Okay, kiddies, we need a quorum! Do we let this slug-a-bed play possum, or do we give him the Waikiki treatment?"

"The treatment!" they echoed, to plenty of hoots and catcalls.

I'm on *Candid Camera*, Harry thought, as someone yanked his blankets away.

"Oooh, *boxers!*" cried a dozen honeymooners, the shock of their voices unmistakable. "He's got on boxer shorts!"

There was nowhere to hide. "I—I was going to pack pajamas," Harry began, but when he raised up and opened his eyes, the words caught in his throat. His jaw might have been missing a hinge. "Holy cow!" he said. He had never seen so many naked people in one place.

"What are you, a nonconformist?" asked the cricket man, actually a rotund, middle-aged fellow with a part down the center of his scalp that seemed to match the part in his chest hair and the fur circling his rounded belly. Even naked, he was the neatest man Harry had ever seen.

"I'm not really . . . anything," Harry tried to explain. "I mean, I'm here for my father, Bernie Finnegan. He's over there, in—"

"Bernie!" chirped the neatly parted fellow. "Of course! You must be his son, Harry! I'm Chuck Burnell, director here. . . ."

"Pleased to meet you," said Harry, trying hard to act casual. He struggled to sit up in the water bed so he could shake hands. "So this is a nudist colony, huh?"

"No, no, no!" cried Burnell, his voice getting even more insect-like. He reddened and made pudgy little fists. "We can't call it an *N* camp. Don't even say the word! It's a zoning thing. We've got to list as a cloth-ing-op factory. Strictly clothing op! Otherwise, the chamber of commerce boys shut us down *like that*. Most folks who move in just decide not to *op*, if you get my meaning."

"Of course." There were a few throat clearings and titters, and Harry tugged self-consciously at the elastic around his waist. He tried not to look at the director's privates, which hooked to the left, or at the hummocky thighs of the older ladies. The problem was finding somewhere to aim his eyes, and he finally settled on his own feet. "I'm really just here to be with my dad," Harry explained. "I don't really know if it's a nude kind of situation."

"That's *clothing optional!*" steamed Burnell, coloring up again. "I told you!"

"That's what I meant," Harry said, still staring at his toes. "I think it's more of a clothes-on situation than a clothes-off, at least for now."

There was some murmuring among the newlyweds, and Harry lifted his eyes cautiously. The entire predicament was so peculiar, Harry almost forgot he was still sprawled in his underwear, on display for a horde of senior sun worshipers.

"All righty," cackled a gaunt gentleman as he bounced a volleyball off the bungalow floor. "Me 'n' m' buttercup feel like doin' some spikin'," he cackled again, jiggling his Adam's apple. "Come on, 'mooners!"

One by one, the Waikiki newlyweds trooped back out of Spicecake. Only Burnell stayed behind long enough to say how sorry he was about Harry's dad and that he hoped the old guy would pull through. "Around here, we call him the Walter Winchell of Waikiki Haven," he chuckled. "I guess you could say he's got a little scoop on just about all of us."

Harry smiled and thanked him, wondering if what he'd just heard was good or bad, when the well-groomed nudie chief stopped at the door and spun around. "You want my advice, son, can the skivvies. When in Rome, there's no point acting Armenian—if you get my drift."

"Loud and clear," said Harry, tugging the blankets back over his head the second the man was out of sight.

An hour or so later, Finnegan made his move.

By sneaking out of Spicecake, keeping to the back of Baked Alaska and flitting through the jonquils that bordered the shuffleboard courts, he managed to make it to his dad's without meeting any nakeds. Only once, skirting the wading pool, did he nearly bump head on with a family of clothing ops. Crouched by a Dumpster, he spied on the clan, three generations from bent and heavy-chested grandma to acned teen, as they trotted off for a dip. Harry wondered if they were year-rounds or if they just went bare when they visited. He could not imagine flapping around with his own wife. Marge did not even like to undress in front of him—after twelve years of marriage, she still disrobed in the closet. And try as he might, he could not bring himself to head off without any clothes on. Instead, he wore the boxers he'd slept in, a baggy pair Marge had bought him for the bicentennial, stamped with little flags and Lincolns.

Approaching the bungalow the back way, he heard his father's voice and stopped under the window to listen. "Sure," the old man was going on, "reminds me of the time Dino, Lawford, and Frankie were skinny-dipping at the Sands. Must've been sixty, sixty-two. Anyway, out comes the manager, and he says, 'Sorry, folks, pool's closed.' Can you imagine? Half the pack's out there doin' belly flops in the altogether, and he makes the payin' customers hit the pavement! Those were the days, boy. Rob Roys by the *tureen*. We ran a feature about it in the June ish. . . . Raised all kinds of stink."

Still stooping, Harry scooted around to the front and took a deep breath. It had been two years since he'd seen his father, and his heart was thumping.

"Daddy," Harry blurted as he burst through the doorway. "It's me! It's your son, Harry!"

The old man looked up momentarily, then went back to the cards he held in his hand as he sat in bed. "Have a seat, kiddo, I'm almost gin. Two cards and I take these *putzes* to the cleaners."

"Okay," said Harry, and he dropped onto a barstool by the door.

For a moment, he thought he was going to weep, but he steadied himself with a peek around the room. Flanking his dad's bed were two naked old guys, one a thin, brittle-looking fellow with liver spots dotting his back, the other a squat, bullish man with bushy side-burns and a Twisted Sister headband. "Joe Alzheimer," announced the brittle fellow with a friendly wave, "no relation to the disease."

"And I'm Greenstein," the bushy chum called over his shoulder. "Stateside, I'm known as the Chaise Lounge King. You might've seen my ads. Stores in all forty-eight big ones, except Utah. Don't ask me why. My theory is, Mormons don't like to recline."

"Harry don't wanna hear all that," his father inter-jected, slamming down a three of clubs. "He's an important coupon guy back in Chi town. You probably

read his stuff: REDEEMABLE AT THE TIME OF PUR-
CHASE. VOID WHERE PROHIBITED. Harry writes that
stuff. He's got no time for lawn furniture."

"Wow," said Alzheimer, "you don't look a minute
over forty, either. That sounds like a heck of a respon-
sibility for a guy just over forty."

Harry, who happened to be thirty-four, again
fought off the urge to bury his face in his hands. "Nice
to meet you," he said and managed to smile. He knew
his dad was doing his best to build him up. But nothing could disguise the fact that banging out SAVE $1 ON
YOUR NEXT NABISCO PURCHASE! was a thousand times
less thrilling than scooping Earl Wilson on the Cary
Grant-Luba Otasevic scandal. Back in '59, Bernie
Finnegan had beat out the pack on the leading man's
fling with the lady hoopster—and had dined out on it
for years. But even worse for Harry was the fact that
he'd dropped everything to fly off and be with his
dying father, and here was the old guy telling Vegas
stories and winning at gin rummy. Just like he always
did. "You're not supposed to be having fun, you're supposed to be dying!" he felt like saying, but bit his
tongue. What kind of son would even think of such a
thing?

The oxygen tent had been folded back over the
headboard, and Bambi now perched beside her husband, as naked as a waif, fanning the old man with a
giant banana leaf. When Harry caught her eye, she
shook her head sadly, as though what they were wit-

nessing were death throes, not a guy and his pals in a penny-a-point gin game. Harry was so out of sorts, he could not even focus on the girl's body, beyond reflecting that her breasts were colossal for someone so petite.

The bed tray on which they were playing was propped over his dad's middle and sounded a resounding *thwack* every time one of the fellows discarded. With each slap, Harry grew a little more agitated. He was about to leap and say something, but just then his dad yelled, "I'm a ginny!" and broke into a coughing fit that had all three men scrambling to smack him on the back. When he started gagging, Bambi slapped an oxygen mask across his mouth. The tank was tucked beside the bed for easy access. After a second more, his father waved them off, but Harry quickly regretted his thoughts of a second earlier.

"Maybe we oughta take a break," said Bambi, and both boys nodded that they understood.

"Sure thing," said Alzheimer. "See ya later, Bern. And nice to meet *you*," he added, turning to shake hands with Harry before leaving.

But Greenstein, the Chaise Lounge King, hung on a moment longer. "Check it out," he barked, pointing to the Twisted Sister sweatband around his head. He wore his few remaining strands of hair swept forward, covering the top of his skull from somewhere around his occiput. "This is 'cause you gotta keep up with the kids. Me 'n' your daddy see eye to eye on that. You're only as young as you feel!" Here he snapped into a quick frug around the bed, sneaking a pinch at Bambi's bottom and frugging back again. "And this doll here feels pretty young to me!" he hooted.

"Hey, none of that," snarled Finnegan's dad. "Find your own."

"Sure, sure," chuckled Greenstein, poking Harry in the ribs. "I love this guy! He's got the best broad in the joint and he won't even let his pals have a pinch."

When the old man felt well enough, he handed the tube back to the girl and asked if she'd mind running out for magazines. "I still keep up," he explained, "even though this *People* crap is nothing like the old days. I don't trust any magazine that don't use composites." His eyes misted over and he got a kind of far-off look. "One month, we must've pasted Ingrid Bergman next to every chump who ever got off a bus at Hollywood and Vine. That was the same ish we ripped the lid off Kookie—'Mad Ave. makes millions off kiddie comb craze' . . . Edd Byrnes claims, 'Mom always told me to look neat!' *Edd Byrnes!* Those were the days, boy."

Finnegan had heard it all before but wanted to make his dad happy any way he could. "That must've been something huh?"

"Don't patronize me," growled his father, and Harry felt instantly crushed. You couldn't win with the guy, which is one reason he'd stayed away as long as he had. "Grab me a *Midnight*, a *Star*, and an *Enquirer*," the old man told Bambi as she fished in her purse. "And pick up some Coppertone for Harry. He's not going to be prancing around in those shorts for long, and there's nothing worse than an ass burn the first day out."

Harry was embarrassed at being treated this way in front of the girl, but Bambi just smiled as she scampered off. After she left, Bernie Finnegan nodded proudly. He moved the tray off his midsection, exposing his old-guy organ to his son, who'd never really seen it before.

"So what do you think?"

"Well," said Harry, a little flustered, "it doesn't *look* sick."

"Not that," snapped his father. "I mean my *bambina*. My B.W. She's some stepmother, huh? Guys'd kill for a little somethin' like that in the family."

"*Dad!*" Harry blushed.

With some effort, his father propped himself up on his elbows, and up close Harry saw for the first time how sick he really was. He'd grown so thin, the cords in his neck stuck out painfully. And the slightest exertion set him panting. Even the tattoo on his shoulder—loose talk, in scarlet filigree—had faded to a greenish blur, like some kind of label that had gone through the wash once too often.

"Kid," his dad began, his voice now no more than a rasp, "there's two things you oughta know about your old man. I'm dying and I'm broke. Bustereeno. I wanted to get you down here to hear it straight from me, so you don't find out the hard way."

"But, Dad . . . I mean, you look—"

"Like Georgie Jessel on his last *Merv*," his father butted in. "I happened to catch the show. Guy looked like he was on leave from the mortuary. Sonny boy, a bum tater's a bum tater. Believe me. They've done everything to my weenie but roast it on a stick. The chemo, the shmeemo, the operations, the examinations where they make you bend over and play *up periscope* while they talk about their golf game. I tell ya, Harry, I don't see how these guys hold their lunch."

"Come on, Pop," Harry pleaded. "You're doing okay."

"Would you knock it off? As if the dingus isn't bad enough, I need a rest every minute and a half from the emphysema. Don't get me wrong, I'm not complaining. I've had some laughs. But if I don't say what I have to say now, you might have to wait till after the next nap, and who knows . . . you know what I mean?"

Harry had never learned how to handle his dad's dramatics and just tried not to acknowledge them. He moved to the seat at the head of the bed, where the ailing gossip grabbed his knee for leverage.

"Slide me against the wall," he said, and Harry eased him backward.

Finnegan Sr. flattened one hand to his chest and sucked in enough air for another sentence. Harry had a feeling he needed the oxygen again but did not want to admit it until he had said what he had to.

"Daddy," Harry said softly, but his father waved him off.

"Don't 'Daddy' me, kid. I'm a pro. I made my living sniffing out crap. I know your mother and you never approved of me. But bereft as I am—which reminds me, you'll be getting the bill for this fun house the second I croak; my apologies—bereft as I am, I still want to leave you a little something. I want to make it up to you for all the times I was off carousing when you were stuck home with your mother, may she rest in one piece."

Harry opened his mouth, but the words came out in a soft moan. "What is it?"

"What it is," said his father, brightening considerably, "is Bambi. I want to leave you Bambi."

"*You what?*"

"Tit for tat," cackled his dad. "I only wish my old man had left me something that nice. All I got from that crumb bum was a Purple Heart he didn't even earn—he got it in a crap game."

"But . . . *Bambi*," Harry sputtered. "I don't—"

"You don't what?" The color had returned to his father's cheeks. He looked almost young again. "I didn't even have to sell her," he declared, as if this were the best part of all. "I just dropped a hint about a week ago, after my last checkup, and she said it was A-OK, as long as she got to stay here in Waikiki. You can come on down and visit when you want to, or you can move right in."

"Dad, *I'm married!*" The pleading in Harry's voice surprised him, as if he were begging his father to write him a note so he could get out of it. "I'm a married man."

"Of course you are—and you're gonna stay that way! When it comes to man and wife, Bernie Finnegan says you got to honor the office. Look at Jack Kennedy. No matter where he was planting it, Jackie stayed up on that pedestal. That's class! You think I ever caused your mother grief?" He paused when he saw his son's expression. "Okay, maybe a little. But only by accident! Your father always took care of the home front. He honored the office!"

Harry started to say something, but the old man waved him off again. He had worked himself up. A thick vein quivered in his temple, and his face shone a boiled-tomato color. He began taking tiny gasps between each word, but nothing could stop him.

"Kiddo, we talked about it. Last night, after she showed you around, she woke me up to tell me how much she likes you. She *likes* you, buddy boy, and Bambi ain't a gal that likes easy, believe me. That mug Greenstein said he'd sign over his El Dorado—*for one night*—and she laughed in his face."

"Maybe she wanted it for more than a night," said Harry, setting his father off with a rasping snort that turned into a wheeze, then worked its way into a hacking cough. He sounded like a bad clutch.

"Always a kidder," gasped the old man. "You're such a kidder, I don't know why you never did *Merv* along with Jessel." He coughed again, doubling up this time.

"You should make half what that man left to his damn poodle with what you make writing coupons for feminine napkins."

"Not that again," said Finnegan wearily. Months ago, Bambi had spotted a 30 CENTS OFF slip in a Modess box, and she asked Harry on the phone if his firm had handled it: "That happens to be one of mine," he told her, in a flush of authorial pride, and had regretted it ever since.

"Okay, I'm teasing," said his father, catching his breath. "That's a good-looking coupon. I couldn't be prouder."

"Dad, please," said Harry, but in another second he'd started gagging again. This time, he motioned for his son to grab the oxygen.

"Right . . . there," the old man panted, and Harry reached over to try to turn the valve on top of the little tank. "No," he gasped, but Harry was still wrestling with the valve and didn't hear. He tried frantically to turn the dial and finally tipped the whole thing over, crashing the night table with his father's Sony and his Snoopy clock radio. But the old man didn't notice. By now, his eyes bulged and his face throbbed purple. The sweat ran in black streaks down his cheeks from all that polish. At last, he got out a single word—"mask"—and Harry caught on. He grabbed the oxygen mask and his father snatched it and shoved his face inside. Clutching it with both hands, he inhaled until his shoulders hunched up around his ears.

"Harry," his father whispered when he was able, "it was already *on.* . . ."

"Oh, Jesus," Finnegan groaned. "I'm sorry. . . ."

But the old gossip dismissed him with a kindly wave. "Relax, pally. Just wake me up for the luau."

Then he crossed his legs and keeled over on the water bed, as dapper as ever.

Harry decided to spend the three days before the funeral right there in Waikiki Haven. At first, he was uneasy about the prospect of a nude funeral. But after the very first day, it made more sense. He and Bambi really got to know each other. The girl informed him that his father had wanted to be cremated and to have his ashes scattered in the flowers around the shuffle-board courts. He'd jotted down a few little plans for the occasion that he, Bambi, and Chuck Burnell went over ahead of time. The idea was to have a modest cere-mony there at the courts around nine, then ease into a light brunch and kick off the first annual Bernie Finnegan Memorial Shuffleboard Classic at noon on the dot. When Harry called Marge with the news, he left out the brunch-and-shuffleboard part and men-tioned instead that he wanted to cash in his return ticket and use the credit to give her an extra week in Bora Bora. Marge was overwhelmed with this generos-ity. "Except when will *you* be coming back?" she kept asking, but Harry told her to just enjoy herself and they'd talk about that later, which seemed to do the trick.

The morning of the ceremony, Harry spent a long while in front of the cabana mirror, deciding how to wear his black arm band. Since "nudists have no lapels," as Burnell explained, traditional clothing-op mourning-wear consisted of black armbands for men and black mantillas for the ladies. Finnegan finally decided on sliding the band high up on his right biceps, gladiator style, and at eight-forty-five sharp, he and Bambi stepped out of Spicecake and headed for the shuffleboard courts.

The young widow wore a veil over her face and black spike heels, a combo the bereaved son had a feeling he'd be requesting for years to come—all thanks to his dad's inimitable foresight and generosity.

About sixty nakeds—the entire Haven population, barring the grounds crew, who insisted on keeping their civvies on and shunned contact with live-ins— showed up for Bernie Finnegan's service.

The sky shone cheery blue and an easy breeze blew from the east. Harry stepped up, ashes in hands, and gave a nod all around before beginning his modest eulogy. "Der Bingle, Danny Thomas, Bob Hope," he intoned. "Just about everybody my dad admired had a tournament named after him. And now he's finally got one of his own."

"We just hope, wherever he is, he can peek down and enjoy it," Bambi chimed in, as planned, and then

Finnegan unscrewed the lid from the urn the mortician had given him. A hush fell over the crowd, and there were a few sniffles as he began to scatter his father's ashes here and there alongside the asphalt courts. But just then the breeze picked up, and some of the grit blew in the direction of the nudists, who squinted and brushed themselves.

"Do you realize," cried Bumell, "if we had pants on, this stuff would be landing in our cuffs?"

"Holy cow, you're right!" said Finnegan.

He felt certain, as the last bits drifted off in the wind, that he had made the right decision.

# TWILIGHT OF THE STOOGES

It's 1980-something. I'm nowhere.

Suzy, this older white lady I buy cocaine from, tells me she'll give me a free gram if I help her do some.

I say, "Sure, why not?"

She says, "Exactly." Then, before my eyes, she gets on her hands and knees on the cat pee-marinated shag carpet. She raises the salmon nightie she lives in, exposing a pair of sixty-three-year-old, weirdly hot, baby-smooth cheeks, which she introduces as Heckel and Jeckel's albino cousins. Jiggling her ass cheeks the way body builders will jiggle their pecs, left-right-left, she makes them talk to each other.

"Heckel likes to get spanked. Bad little crow!"

"Jeckel, you're such a freak."

After fifteen minutes, or maybe a day, Suzy pretends to get annoyed with her chatty buttocks. She tells them to shut up. As I zone in and out, grinning like I haven't seen Miss Chatty Cheeks five thousand times already, I am simultaneously wondering how long I can go without asking/begging/stealing another hit, and obsessing on the name of the guy who did Topo Gigio on *Ed Sullivan*.

*By the time I write this, I am acutely aware of how old remembering* The Ed Sullivan Show *makes me. Tennessee Williams routinely shaved a year off his age. When people caught him he'd explain that he didn't count the year he worked in a shoe store. I sometimes think the same could be done with drug years. They don't count. Though probably they count more. Like dog years. My liver, in point of fact, is well over a hundred. It sometimes forgets its own name and will doubtless be placed to rest in a home by the time you read this.*

Suzy's TV is always on with the sound off. After a while you begin to think the rays soak into your head and over the blood brain barrier with the rest of the shit you're putting in there. Suzy resembles Miss Hathaway, Mr. Drysdale's horsy secretary on *The Beverly Hillbillies*—if Miss Hathaway had been locked in a dark room and force-fed Kents, cocaine, and gin for twenty-seven years, while bathed in color Sony light.

She reaches back and hands me a straw, a regular Sweetheart, with red stripes down the side. "Okay, soldier, pack some in there."

"In the straw?"

"In my *ass*. Jesus! How dumb are you? Put some powder in the straw, put the straw in my ass, and blow."

"I've done worse for less," I say with a shrug, trying to convey an emotion I do not even remotely feel. In fact, there is actual screaming in my head, a voice that sounds alarmingly like Jimmy Swaggart. (More TV-adjacent damage; I might as well be in the box, getting transmissions directly into my pineal gland.) I am never not awake Sunday morning at four, when Jimmy comes on in my neck of the world.

*Am I nervous or am I happy?*
*Why are you staring?*
*Fuck, HELICOPTERS!*

Right before I angle toward the target, I start to feel chiggers under my skin, and I fight the urge to scratch myself bloody digging them out. This is when I hear Jimmy Swaggart start speaking directly to me: "Hey, loser! You're about to blow drugs into the anus of a woman old enough to be your mother. You know what Jesus says about that?"

Happily, I am so cocaine depleted I instantly forget that I'm aurally hallucinating, and that I itch. You don't know you're having a white-out until you come out of it. I just kind of *blink to*. I remember that I'm trying to keep my thumb pressed on one end of the straw while I slip the other end in Suzy's pink O without spilling any coke. (Her sphincter, for reasons I can't fathom, makes me think of a dog toy.) I hold my breath, mouth poised by the business end of the tube, the length of a *TV Guide* away from the bull's eye. I have a weird pain in my spleen. Though I'm not sure where my spleen is. I just know it's unhealthy. And I should go to a dentist, too. I can only chew with the left rear corner of my mouth.

"When I say do it, *do* it!" Suzy says, and launches into some kind of Kundalini fire-breathing that expands and puckers her chosen coke portal. For one bad moment I am eyeball to eyeball with a jowly, Ray Harryhausen Cyclops, who won't stop leering at me. Then I avert my gaze and take in the pictures of Suzy's dead B-celebrity husband on the wall. The Teddy Shrine . . . *that's better*. Suzy met her late husband when she was a call girl. (Many of her clients were half-washed-up New York stage actors.) In a career lull, Teddy appeared in a number of *Three Stooges* vehicles. But not, as Suzy would interject when she repeated the story—which she did *no more than ten times a night*— "the good *Three Stooges* . . ." Teddy made his Stooge ascendance in the heyday of Joe DeRira, the Curly-replacement nobody liked. "Twilight of the Stooges," Suzy would sigh. "People even liked Shemp better than they liked DeRita."

Suzy worked a finite loop of peripheral celebrity anecdotes. . . . Bennett Cerf liked to be dressed like a baby and have his diaper changed. . . . Broderick Crawford liked to give girls pony rides. Goober from

*Andy Griffith* was hung like a roll of silver dollars but had a dime-size hole burned in his septum. She also claimed that her apartment on Ivar, a cottage cheese–ceilinged studio a short stagger up from Franklin, used to belong to Nathanael West. I can still see her tearing up, missing a dear friend: "The midget from *Day of the Locust* died the same day John Lennon was shot."

I spent more time with Suzy than my own wife, which is a whole other story. After a certain point, junkies are rarely missed when they're not home. (If they happen to have a home—as opposed to a place they still have keys to, from which they can steal small appliances.)

A half-second before I think she is ready to blast off, Suzy abruptly turns around and chuckles. "I ever tell you how much Larry Fine loved his blow? The man was a hedonist. . . . How do you think his hair got that way? He wanted to be the white Cab Calloway but it never worked out."

Luckily I don't spill anything. Did I mention the white-outs? I did, didn't I? Why am I telling this story? It's not even a story. It's just, like, a snippet from a loop. Like Suzy's bottom-feeding monologues. I don't have memories. I just have nerves that still hurt in my brain. Shooting coke does that. Even more than smoking it, when you fixed you could just wipe the inside of your skull clean as porcelain. Coke was about toilets and toi-

lets were shiny white. Especially at 4 A.M. with the
lights on and the bathroom door locked. Sometimes
the blood in your head would crash over your eyeballs
and you'd just go blind for a while, but you wouldn't
notice till you could see again—when you came back
and realized you were standing there, knuckles buck-
ling, one hand propped on the wall, the other compulsively flushing and re-flushing the toilet, for the
whoosh that could make you come.

*I've done okay since getting off all of it—the dope and the
cocaine—but I still think, much as the smack destroyed my
liver, the coke shorted my synapses. All systems will be fir-
ing and then, next thing I know, I'll blink into vision again
and realize I've gone blank. It's not so much as if the power's
been diminished, it's as if the power just suddenly . . . goes out.
Can we feel anything as sharply as the absence of a specific
feeling?*

*What the fuck does that mean?*

*What was I just talking about?*

*Never mind. It's not coming back.*

*When I think about getting high, what I remember, vis-
cerally, is not the heroin rush—those faded years before I
stopped the heroin—I remember the coke hitting, that fork-
in-the-heart jolt, like you dipped your toe in a puddle and
tongue-kissed a toaster.*

*Before the needle was halfway down, you could see
God's eyes roll back in His head.*

So I twitch back and there's this gaping Eberhard Faber eraser-colored hole, two hummocky cheeks yanked open, scarlet chipped fingernails against baby skin.

"Hey, Whitey Ford, throw the dart through the hula hoop, dammit! What's the puzzle!?"

So (first time's always the hardest) with no further ado, I stick the straw into Suzy's ass, careful not to inhale, and blow the Pixie Stix's worth of flake into her alimentary canal, or whatever it is, and watch the teeny mouth shut tight around its deposit.

Suzy squirms. "Ungggghh-uhhhh . . . oh God . . . *NNNNNNGGGGGG!*"

Then she twists her head around, glassy-eyed. "*I'm a regular Venus flytrap!*"

That's when I realize I left the straw in her. I look everywhere but it's gone. Sucked right up with the blow. Should I tell her? Would she get mad when she found out? What if she cut me off? Or was there some kind of ass-acid that could eat a straw to pulp—so she'd never know?

Suzy mistakes my panic and paralysis for awe. "Impressive, right?" Smacking herself on the flank, she adds, "I used to smuggle guns for the Panthers in there. There's a man named Jackson who could tell you some stories, if he was in a position to tell anybody anything."

Then she giggles, doing a little wiggly thing with her bottom. "A lot of guys paid a lot of money to be where you are right now! Now blow some more, Daddy. Blow! Blow! Blow!"

I reload from a Musso & Franks ashtray full of powder and go in for Round Two. Her capacious anus quivers like some blind baby bird. And this time (with a fresh straw) I close my eyes, unload the blow, then quickly get up and weave into the bathroom to shake up a shot. I should put some dope in but can't find it— and can't wait—and before I have the needle out I'm on the floor, doing the floppy-fish. It takes everything I have to slap a chunk of tar on tin foil and take a puff to stop the convulsion. I make it back out to the living room. (Blinds always pulled, no day or night, like a one-woman keno lounge.) I never saw Suzy get off her couch to pee. I never saw her eat. I never saw her do anything but cocaine, generally up her nose—or, on special occasions, the odd ass-blow.

Suzy didn't geeze, she thought it was low class. She left the freebasing to her roommate, Sidney, a shut-in who could generally be found in his room, sniffing a pillow between hits. Sidney hadn't left his room, Suzy liked to say, since *The Rockford Files* was new. His claim to fame was playing drums behind Lenny Bruce at a Detroit strip club.

I didn't have any money, so I would keep Suzy company. I never had to be anywhere.

Suzy is still talking when I come back from the bathroom. She never stopped talking. It was not quite white noise, Suzy's clients were a talk show host, a couple of soap stars, a slew of jingle musicians, one name actor who required oz's mailed to him on the set, and my favorite, a TV evangelist famous for his high-rise hair and his multi-hour rants from a cowhide chair in Pasadena.

"I know what you're thinking."

Suzy's voice is jagged with pleasure. Her nose so permanently blown out she sounds like she's just unplugged her iron lung. "You're thinking, 'Suzy musta stole the ass-blow move from Stevie Nicks.' Well, you're wrong, baby. It's apocryphal. Stevie Nicks kept a guy on the payroll whose only job was to blow coke up her ass. Well, not his only job. His other job was to make sure she didn't stop for KFC on the way back from a concert. She'd put a broken nail file to her throat if the driver didn't stop for a half dozen nine-piece boxes. She was a chicken hoover, if you know what I mean."

"I know what you mean."

"I know you know," Suzy says, lowering her nightie, squirming with pleasure as she eases her behind back on the couch.

"Did I ever tell you about the time Larry got Shemp drunk and they put a hooker's eye out in Canter's?"

*Only five thousand times.*

"I never heard that one."

"Here, have some more."

Years go by.

# PURE

*My vagina is a gift from Jesus. The Lord made me holy this way. Hallelujah!*

Anyone listening would hear her murmur. Below words. The way prayer is below words. In the mouth, but really in the heart.

*And in my pants.*

She'd taken the virginity pledge four years ago, after Laura Bush came to visit her high school and opened a white First Lady bible to First Thessalonians 4:3-4. "God wants you to be holy, so you keep clear of all sexual sin." She still wore her silver chastity ring to remind her, in the face of temptation, that pure attracts pure.

*Believing that true love waits, I make a commitment to God, myself, my family, and my future mate to a lifetime of purity and sexual abstinence from this day until the day I enter a biblical marriage relationship.*

When Christ returns, abstinents will have the first seat on the chariot to salvation.

****

She caught four reds in a row on Vanowen and each time snuck a peek at herself in the rearview of her vintage Falcon. The blue contacts were working. So was the wig. Valley men all wanted blue-eyed blondes. Most guys did. Pastor Bob, the founder of Christian Fun Girls, her agency, told her this one sounded like some Colonel Klink, from *Hogan's Heroes*. Pastor Bob wasn't just the owner. He took calls and screened for freaks.

"Said he was a *'dok-tor,'*" the pastor giggled. This tickled the socks off him, even though every other guy who called for a date claimed to be a doctor—as though the medical profession, or the pretense, were some kind of anti-scam hex.

Besides MD's, lots of young guys liked to say they were military. This was a tell they were going to pull some "On Leave from Falujah" routine and ask for a discount. The soldier boys all made the same joke when she wouldn't let them touch her *down there*. "What'sa matter honey, you Al Qaeda?"

She didn't like to think of them as tricks. She preferred the term "love partners," as Jan and Paul Crouch called folks who dialed in and pledged on the love line that flashed on the crawl beneath their plush *Praise the Lord* chairs on the Trinity Broadcasting Network. When she got older, she wanted Bo Peep hair like Jan's.

*15288 Hamlin—where the h-e-double-lemon drops is that?*

Christian love partners could be animals, just like heathens. *Thank you, Jesus.* You'd think the Hollywood types, especially the wannabe Hollywood types, would come on the pushiest. Huh-uh. Turned out they were the most sheepish. Apologetic about where they lived. Compelled to explain they were "between projects"— or to show them their awards. She'd seen the same Emmy—it had a weird bulge in the middle—often enough to know it came from the pawnshop on Vanowen and Rodney. Where, legend had it, Danny Bonaduce had deposited dozens after having them manufactured in a factory in Tijuana. Not, apparently, having won one of the trophies himself. She'd been in the pawnshop more than once, when the Lord was trying her financial faith, and always spotted at least one of the tumored statuettes.

Church-going men weren't half as nervous as the ones in show business. Rapture-hounds didn't pretend to be righteous. If they were born again, even thirty-plus "mouches"—half men, half couches who still lived at home—wanted to feel the sin. It made them brave. It didn't matter if they had to ply their dying mothers with Valium and gin to get some privacy. They had that righteous confidence. *Praise be!* She'd once serviced a room full of Promise Keepers in an Anaheim Holiday Inn, and to a man they'd understood—they'd *appreciated*—her vaginal hands-off policy. Saw the silver ring on her finger and knew. The ones who didn't want to worship-lick her wanted to spank her, and then apologize. But it was the apology that got them off. One of Promise Keepers was an ex-linebacker for the Cowboys. When he took off his shirt she saw his six-pack and she felt a quickening. Heard the devil's whisper. *Maybe it's time to re-think this silver ring thing.* But all the Cowboy wanted to do was talk. He had a high, halting voice, and talked like he was trying to figure out the meaning of everything he said at the same time he was saying it. "Mommy knew what Daddy was doing and she didn't stop it! . . ." *Sounds like somebody needs a cuddle.* What else could she say?

She caught herself zoning and eyed the rows of apartment complexes, what girls at the agency called loser barracks, because so many outcall customers lived in them, along with the divorced and abandoned single moms and their broods.

Spotting 15288, she eased to the curb, in front of the VACANCY sign. A chain slung between two posts on the lawn held up the graffitied announcement: RENTING NOW—BACHELORS AVAILABLE! The exclamation point, no doubt, was there to convey the excitement any bachelor would feel about moving in. The place was identical to thousands of others, all over the San Fernando Valley: two stories of painted-over cinderblock, sky blue washed out to dirty white, the swimming pool visible through the glass double doors in front. High on the faded wall above them, in a kind of carefree, 1960s-ish, come-on-in-and-live-the-dream California swirl, was the name the original owners had given the building: SEA BREEZE APARTMENTS.

The Pacific Ocean was twenty-seven miles away, which is still a lot closer than it is to Cleveland.

Before leaving the car, she snapped open her purse, fished around for her blessing matches, found them and pulled them out for a strength-giving gander. For a long moment, she let her eyes rest on the on the front of the matchbook, where JIMP was spelled in letters that looked like the kind of the Ten Commandments. These stood for the first four words of Pastor Bob's special escort prayer. Slowly, she repeated the words to herself: *Jesus is my pimp, I shall not freelance. . . . He maketh me lie down in Motel Sixes. . . .*

It was funny, but not just.

JIMP got started when Pastor Bob switched up the thirteenth psalm during a prayer circle at Love House, the sober living where all the agency girls lived. (The US government gave him money for promoting abstinence, and California subsidized him for the price of rehab beds.) Instead of "the Lord is my shepherd," he busted out "Jesus is my pimp!" and everybody fell out. Mandy, Earline, Faith-Based Tina, Lee-Anne, Randi . . . they all worked for Pastor Bob. And they all knew what he did before he got sentenced to a nickel in Quentin, which is where is the Lord appeared in the chow line and told him to minister to fallen women. *If Jesus was in lock-down, he'd turn the water into pruno.*

None of the girls at the agency talk about politics or anything. All we talk about is Jesus and sex. Sometimes—I shouldn't even say this—we talk about sex with Jesus. I mean, when you think about it, we are saving ourselves for Him, right? We say it's for our husband—*Oh, goodie, a beefy UPS man with butt acne!*—but we keep the secret desire in our hearts. If He comes back, there are going to be a lot of excited girls. Jesus groupies. Of course, there are rapture hags, divorcées who develop engine trouble in megachurch parking lots after the service; Bible sluts who get drunk and orgy with Tim LaHaye imitators at *Left Behind* conventions. *Folks, Tim couldn't be here today, he had a family matter he had to minister to. But we've got somebody I think you're gonna like....* (Not to judge. I once came to in a Winnebago with a little person named Tink LaHaye. He had a comedy ministry. And the whole RV was crammed with stacks of his publicity photos. He had a book he sold after the show. *Left Behind— and Under the Table!: The Inspiring Life Story of God's Littlest Giant.* One thing, though: it's true what they say about "little people.")

Here's the dirty little secret: sometimes, when a Christian girl says she is waiting for the right man, she means Jesus. There I said it. That's the hottie we're all waiting for. God's hunky Son!

How do I know there *is* a God? That He is working in my life? Well, before I took the pledge—this was still high school!—I was *this* close to giving it up to Norbert, my biker boyfriend, until I saw the two thunderbolts tattooed where his pubes would be. *WHITE POWER!* (But not much of it, if you know what I mean.) Of course I didn't need to make a vow of chastity to pass on Norb. (What kind of dude shaves his pubeys? *Hello!*) But after Norbert, I began to feel different. Inside. Way inside. Like I said, I went to a Teens for Jesus rally at my high school and saw Mrs. Bush and that's when I decided. *No más.* This didn't mean I stopped going out. Just the opposite. The very next week I went down on three boys in one night. (They played in this Christian punk band, Hate-Love). I let the drummer do me *back there.* Though I admit I partook of illegal substances—and still do, sometimes—I still saved myself. I stayed *pure.* Because I knew, no matter what I did, what I *didn't* entitled me to a sky ride come the apocalypse.

I'd be raptured. But *not just.* The abstinent get early admission. *Praise the Lord.* Straight to the cloud party. I fantasized that, as I was flying up into heaven, I would be able look down and see all the motel boyfriends and eight-ball holders I'd let in into my "lesser portal," as Aileen Dusey, "Queen of the Christian Romance Novel," calls the rear end of a Christian girl in my favorite book: *I'm Not Saying No to You, I'm Saying Yes to Jesus.*

I memorized this passage, which still gets shivers. *"This dark entry, my love, is as coarse as earth itself. But, let it not be forgotten, this dewy forest you seek to enter leads to the womb. And the Holy of Holies belongs to Him . . ."*

Pastor Bob ministered to all the girls who worked for his agency. He passed the prayer matches out so they could have them on hand. To study on and buttress faith in touchy situations. *Jesus is my pimp*, she repeated again as she gathered her bag, stepped out of the Falcon, and locked it manually before heading up the walk to the building's entrance. At first this sounded crass. But now she understood. Only born-again girls in the Life knew what JIMP stood for. Sometimes strangers would see her matches, recognize the letters and raise their hands before them, palms up, in secret recognition. It was like being a Mason who screwed sad men for a living.

PASTOR BOBISM NUMBER ONE:
*Sex is a ministry. Every mortal man is maimed in flesh or spirit. It is our job—and our blessed calling—to help make them whole. Mary Magdalene, the whore, did Jesus' blessed work.*

She paused in front of the building directory and found his name. JOSEPH MINK, MD. Moths flapped around the overhead light, a bare bulb which hummed and sputtered like it was trying to say something. If she was still smoking that tina she'd understand and answer back in *lightbulbese*. If she closed her eyes, she could almost generate the electro-speed *hiss*.

Fucking guys *on* meth made the time pass faster. (Pastor Bob preferred the term "serving." Cursing was discouraged, but sometimes she forgot.) In her first Craigslist ad, before she signed on with the pastor, she said she was "tina-friendly." Lucky a plainclothes didn't show up. Fucking guys *for* meth was different. Nine Armenians at once? Did she do that? *Shrug* . . . after you're awake three days it feels like it's happening to someone else anyway. *Get out of the yesterday basement!* That's what it said on the sign Pastor Bob taped up over door.

PASTOR BOBISM NUMBER TWO:
*Remember, any man you meet may be the Savior. Think of Jesus as that businessman you meet in the lobby of the Airport Radisson. But do NOT begin the Lord's work until the money is in a plain white envelope on a table. If the son of Our Lord comes back as a john in Fontana, he will not be short twenty dollars.*

There was an older whore at the agency named Minna, who looked like Nancy Reagan with knife scars. Her first night going pro-anal, Minna took her aside in the lounge, where the girls sat around watching *The 700 Club* and waiting for calls. "Be careful with the heinie, darlin'. Take hot baths. One Christian gal to another, you don't wanna get the pink glove!"

Minna, who had to be forty, gave her own sagging ass a sad little spank, the way you'd pat a favorite cat you know is going to be euthanized in the morning.

"I'm tellin' you this so my life can be an example, honey. Sometimes, when a man's backin' outa Minna's garage, Minna's tush comes with. Goes inside-out on his thingy, like a pink glove."

"That's awful!" she said. And she meant it.

"It is, Sugar. Sometimes my bee-hind puffs up like a little party balloon. The point is—*STOP IF IT HURTS*. You notice any puff, I don't care if you're in a Jacuzzi with the twelve apostles, you tell 'em to take the party somewhere's else. You get so much as a pang, *N-O spells No*. I didn't say no—now looks at me. I went full NBC five years ago." Minna sniffled and continued, "as in *No Bowel Control*."

She handed Minna a tissue. "Thank you, darlin'. You're a good girl," Minna said "But good ain't enough. You gotta be smart, too. Always bring a box of Kleenex Junior, *and* Handi Wipes, to help spread the Purell. I wish somebody had told me stuff. When I was free-basing that demon cocaine, I spread my nether-globes for any hogleg with a dollar." Dabbing her eyes, Minna looked down at her stomach. She sighed and patted her little tummy-pooch in bittersweet wonder. "Now I'm packin' a poop-bag. . . . For all I know, *I'm goin' right now!*"

That was her big fear: the pink glove. Ever since that talk with Minna, the second she got high, her anus became extra sensitive. Not, like, *pain* sensitive. More like anal paranoia—like *its feelings could be easily hurt*. It was as if her rear end was a grown woman with issues. A vulnerable woman who lived in a dump behind that little do-gooder pussy in the mansion up front. Her buttocks felt as overworked and shunned as Cinderella. As Pastor Bob liked to say: *You ladies have one blessed orifice and one where the Devil makes his home.*

Pastor Bob had another saying, too: *Sometimes the right prayer is a ride out of hell.*

She never had coitus with Pastor Bob. Technically, she'd never had coitus with anybody. Though her aching a-hole begged to differ. She called it her Greek chorus. Ha-ha. Sometimes her asshole wouldn't shut up. *"You think I got that pain from shuffleboard? This sphincter didn't get stretched servin' hot meals to shut-ins, bitch!"* Her ass talked black because it was the baddest part of her. *"Takes more'n Bible study give a bitch's ass this kinda diameter. . . . I'm tired of bein' a ho so you can keep your L'il pinklips pure. Ass ain't s'posed to be a sacrificial lamb. Ass s'posed to be ass!"*

"You be quiet," her untainted womb replied. "That kind of language is not Christian!"

*Lord Jesus, would they ever stop fighting down there?* She remembered she was in public and refrained from answering. But she still wanted to. All that panty chatter made her want to get high, too. She knew she shouldn't. But there was no one around, so she took a quick suck off her one-hitter. When she was really buzzed, she imagined her rear end as a battle-weary German soldier, facing her vagina, a fresh-faced English recruit, foxhole to foxhole across an acrid no man's land. She'd watched lots of History Channel with her daddy. What she loved most was the narrator's virile delivery. *During the worst trench warfare of World War One, thousands died for half an inch of taint.*

*Daddy had a color TV that only got black and white. He pretended it was cool, not having a good TV, like it wasn't because they were poor. Guys fuck the way they wished they could live. That's all it fucking was.*

*That's what she used to think anyway. Before she understood that Jesus loved the harlot most of all.*

Pastor Bob liked to burn CDs of his, and she kept one in her Falcon on the subject of Jesus and foot-washing. *"Man washes a bitch's feet, that's a MAN ain't afraid to act like somethin' LESS'n a man! Jesus act like a foot-washin' little puss, cause he know, he SO MUCH A MAN ain't nobody gonna call him out. . . . Jesus was bad enough to be a bitch, when the situation arose. JC got God-balls, straight up.*

She double-checked the name in the mail slot. If the handle a potential love partner gave did not match the address he'd given, she had to call the agency back and check. Guys liked to use fake names. They had a magic belief that, even after you stepped into *their* homes or *their* hotel rooms—even after they called you on *their* home or cell phones (unblocked numbers only!)—somehow, if they got busted, they'd get off if they said their name was Ed Juke instead of Joe Kallikak. Like that was the loophole in the whole hiring-a-woman-to-have-sex-is-illegal thing. And *they'd* found it!

That fat moth bounced off the lightbulb again with a whizzing thud. People had the whole moth to the flame thing wrong. It was her belief that moths couldn't care less about flames. They were just scared of the dark. She realized, *I am standing here perving on a moth.* Meaning, I'm not thinking about my trash-talking backside. No longer in the grips of anus pain. *Yay God!*

Careful of her nails—Lee Press Ons, since she was always biting her own—she picked up the battered visitor phone and punched one-three-three, then flipped open the blessing matches to stare at the praying hands on the back. Pressed between them, in the matchbook etching, was what looked like Jesus, a penis wearing crown, or a foreshortened unicorn. Depending. It was like that Rorschach test they gave her in juvenile hall, way back.

Her lips moved. Waiting for Joseph Minke, MD to answer, she continued to pray as the cars whooshed past her on Vanowen. Some Cholita, walking by with a pair of pit bulls, laughed into her cell phone, *Yeah you are!*

\*\*\*\*

Take a deep breath. Raise your eyes. For a blazing moment light from above is sweeping over you. An omen! Or actually, a police helicopter. But still . . . come the end times, the four horsemen of the apocalypse might sweep down in LAPD choppers. Pastor Bob said: *The apostles were the first gangbangers. Next time you see somebody make the sign of the cross, tell me it ain't a gang signal.* The lights disappeared. The copters fut-futting into blackness. She heard shuffling. An old man's cough.

"*Ja, Ja,* I'm coming."

She'd never had a German.

*The Apocalypse is gonna be like the best movie that ever was. And if you've accepted Jesus into your heart, you get to see the show AND leave the theater.*

Sometimes the door opened on men so normal they had to be depraved. That could be scary—and scarier because she worked alone. Without a driver. But she was not, she knew, really alone. She had Jesus, whom she imagined in a tank top, with bulging muscles, right there beside her. He had long golden hair like in the Bible pictures. Fabio-hair. Plus Pastor Bob was on speed-dial. In case the Lord had to ordain with a lead pipe.

But still . . . the tweakiest time of all was right now. In two seconds she could be staring at some nice old codger. Or some ex-con crystal freak who's been jack-ing off to *Chicks with Dicks* for three days and forgot he called. Beware the love partner who answers naked in cowboy boots, lotioned up, and thinks the CIA sent you to make him kill his mother.

*Yea though I walk through the condo of meth. . . .*

It felt good to pray. Like it was supposed to.

# ON WATER SHOULDERS

Without knowing why, Morton believed that his parents were imposters. Each night, when his father stepped into the dark bedroom to touch him on the forehead and whisper his love, Morton imagined an unfamiliar face looming above him. He shut his eyes, kept them shut, so the stranger would not know what Morton knew. While large fingers traced his lips, he breathed quietly and pictured the face just inches away. Behind closed lids, he saw the pinched, gross features of the men who huddled on Bogg's Corner and warmed their hands over burning rags in a barrel. His father, he thought, was really one of those men, though he wore gray suits and pretended to come home from work each night.

"What am I thinking?" said Morton's mother in the morning when they played their game. Her eyes puffed out and she was always about to laugh. "I'm in love," she said. She placed Morton in the warm water and leaned close to peck his nose. "I'm in love with the boy who makes little ripples in the tub!"

Morton giggled when she reached under the bubbles. She ran her fingers on the smooth rise between his belly and the downward slope to his thighs. Sometimes Marcella and Elaine, his mother's sisters, would join her in the morning for Morton's bath, and all three would touch him while he squirmed and giggled and felt his bladder go loose in the water with terrible pleasure.

"He's mine, all mine," said his mother. She wrapped Morton in a big towel with clocks and fiddles, and then she passed him to Marcella who squeezed him and called him a little man. Marcella played peek-a-boo through her long red hair. Morton liked her best when she disappeared. For one moment she had no face, and he suffered delicious panic thinking there was really nothing behind her shiny red hair. Morton watched the light playing on all sides of her. He patted her skull, hoping to find nothing but smooth flesh underneath.

In his dream, Morton rode his father's shoulders in the ocean. His father cupped a hand on each of Morton's knees, and as they walked toward the horizon he swooped low and dipped toward the water. Morton tried not to scream. His father always straightened at the last moment, and Morton turned toward the bathers on the beach. Their noise was far away. His father was saying something, and Morton could feel the vibrations of his lungs against his calves.

The words floated by, not quite so important as the shudders in his father's chest when he spoke. Morton towered above the water. From his vantage point the sky wheeled just above him. His father's grip released him, and he looked away from the figures on the beach to the great, bear-shaped clouds. His father was walking with the clouds. At first, water tickled Morton's toes, then it began lapping as far up as his knees. The water swallowed his father to his neck. Looking down, Morton saw his torso squat and uncertain, distorted in the moving ocean.

They came to a rope with brightly colored plastic balls bobbing up and down along its length. Morton's father shifted him to his left arm, then ducked beneath the rope and hoisted him to his right on the other side. Now he was swimming, a solid, unhurried paddle, and Morton rode atop with his hands in the tight curls of his father's neck. He smelled his father's scalp, salt and Old Spice and grease. His legs were cold where they cut through the water. He felt cold and slime against his skin as his father roared into the moving water.

Morton's bedroom was above the garage. At night the lights from his father's car sent a band of red sliding along the ceiling and down the walls. His father had an automatic opener for the garage door. Even before he arrived, Morton felt the deep rumble as the door slowly opened and came to rest in its tracks until his father was safely inside. Morton missed the crunch of his father's car door opening and closing, the solid clicking of his heels on the driveway as he walked the few steps to the garage door to open it himself. Since the new device had been installed, Morton awoke to a rumble, then watched the red tongue slip along above him and in front of him and then disappear.

"Who's my boy?" whispered his father, standing above him, smelling of snow and leather and cigarettes. Morton pretended to sleep. He didn't open his eyes and stiffened at the complex feel of fingers upon his face. Sometimes his father stood beside his bed and breathed heavily for a few minutes before leaving the room.

Each night a different man came to touch him. He heard the rumble, the slam, every now and then the whistle as the person who was his father climbed the steps from the basement to the kitchen, walked to the living room and climbed the steps to Morton's room. When he was once again alone, left with the strange taste of cold in his mouth, Morton heard a splash in the toilet next door and the little laugh his mother gave from the bedroom as she talked with one of her sisters on the phone: "He's home." His mother's voice came to him disembodied, through the window beside his bed. In her room, she lay propped on a TV pillow, chatting next to a window, and the night air carried her side of the conversation, her hilarity, along to his darkness. "He's home. . . . Don't say a word!"

His parents' exchanges took place in the deepest part of the night. Morton was half-awake, pleasantly sliding back after the rumble and his father's cold touch. At first, there were no words: just the clatter of his father's change on the glass dresser-top.

Morton found something to look at in the night sky. He watched the blinking of a red light on a tower. His mother had explained that this was the radar that found lost children. Morton often stared at it through the night, until sleep took him and he saw the dot of blood inside his eyes. The faraway needle was what could rescue you, finally. Morton imagined the scanners locating children everywhere: crouched in doorways, crawling silently on hands and knees through the deserted streets. Even if a child drowned or dropped through a hole the radar could find him. The child-finder rolled its eye and spotted you. If your parents thought you were lost, but you were really only hiding in the basement or in a closet, the big light would turn in troubled revolutions, looking around the world in vain. If you hid in a house, in your own house, then they couldn't find you. If you hid in an obvious place, where they could see you but did not even know you were hiding, if you hid in yourself, that was better.

Morton opened and closed his eyes to see if he could match the on-off blinking of the eye. If he matched, he could open his eyes at perfect intervals and see nothing in the sky, as if the red eye were never there. The same game could be played so that he saw the red dot, so that it always shone, but he never played it that way. He didn't like it. His parents changed out of their masks in the other room when he was not with them, when he turned around they took off their faces. He had simply never blinked at the right time, and never caught them. He opened his eyes, seeing not a trace of the blood light. His rhythm was just right. He closed his eyes and opened them again in pure night.

Morton thought there were clowns inside the walls. He wasn't sure, but behind the closets was another house, a larger one, where Howdy Doody and Clarabelle lived by themselves. One night, Morton drifted down the stairs without touching a single step, like the creatures in the walls. He sat on the carpet beside his father, who sat reading fat books in his yellow chair.

Sometimes Morton heard his mother call from the bedroom for his father: "When are you coming up?" His father liked to read in his chair until very late, and he often fell asleep with his book in his lap, his head tilted to one side, and the lamplight still shining in his glasses. The night Morton drifted down the stairs, his father's eyes were very red. Behind him, the room was in darkness.

His father ran the back of his hand across his chin with a scraping sound that Morton liked. "What are you doing up?" he asked. The lamp glowed behind him, shining so brightly that everything else was black. His father's eyes were dull and red. In the harsh light, alone with his father, Morton remembered no more than that he'd drifted down the stairs. Creatures from TV flitted just beyond the light. The smell of his father's books gave Morton a headache. They were brown and heavy, with gold letters stamped across their wide spines. They were the opposite of the creatures who danced in color where you could not see.

Morton must have gone to sleep beside the chair, his fingers curled in the tassels that hung beneath it. The draft from the stairs knotted his muscles, and he stirred awake with a crick in his neck. His back throbbed. His father's glasses exploded with light. His hand hung cold and swollen over the arm of the chair. They were alone in the light, and Morton touched the black hair on his father's knuckles. He took the hand, which was very heavy, and placed it over his ear, then on top of his head, and then he kissed the solid heart of his father's palm as he stirred and mumbled in his sleep, in the chair beside him.